Please Be Mine Forever

Please Be Mine Forever

NIKITA GUPTA

Srishti
PUBLISHERS & DISTRIBUTORS

Srishti Publishers & Distributors
Registered Office: N-16, C.R. Park
New Delhi – 110 019
Corporate Office: 212A, Peacock Lane
Shahpur Jat, New Delhi – 110 049
editorial@srishtipublishers.com

First published by
Srishti Publishers & Distributors in 2019

10 9 8 7 6 5 4 3 2 1

This is a work of fiction. The characters, places, organisations and events described in this book are either a work of the author's imagination or have been used fictitiously. Any resemblance to people, living or dead, places, events, communities or organisations is purely coincidental.

Printed and bound in India

To my Mom, Dad – who have been a constant support and have helped me turn my dream into a beautiful reality.

To my brother – who, with his brilliance and inventiveness, is an inspiration to me.

To my best friends, uncles and aunts – without their support, this book would only have been an idea.

To all my readers – who always come up with the best ways to encourage me and have boosted me throughout.

Prologue

It was years ago when Aryan found himself drawn towards Chahat. This girl with a golden heart and a contagious smile, couldn't help but fall for this handsome and passionate guy. They didn't realise how, but they ended up meaning the world to each other.

But their present contradicts their past. Because today, after five years, Aryan stands alone, looking for answers of thousands of unanswered questions with Chahat, who had run away from him. With not even a slightest clue behind.

With confused minds, swollen eyes and tired hearts, will Chahat come back to Aryan's – Please be mine forever?

Chahat

December 2014

"Darling! Let's go. We are getting late," Aryan said, standing behind me.

"Yes, love," I responded.

I looked at myself in the mirror for one last time and turned around to face Aryan, who was looking at me with adoration in his eyes. I shoved my tongue at him to which he smiled.

A smile made its way to my lips automatically as I saw him smiling.

Indeed, love is such an astounding feeling. It changes our priorities, our conceptions, and almost everything about us, beyond belief.

"Let's go, you moron!" I sassed.

"That's exactly what I have been saying for the past half an hour, you lazy ass," he teased me back.

"Lazy ass? That was a good one." I laughed.

"I know. I am so talented, baby." He sassed me this time.

"Flatter yourself as much as you like, Mr Kapoor," I said pretending to check my nails.

"Whatever." He huffed and grabbed my hand. I muffled a laugh at his reaction as we left my house to drive towards the wedding destination. Today, my best friend Samaira is getting married to her childhood crush and Aryan's best friend, Siddhant.

"Aryan, I am going to check on Samaira," I said as we reached the destination.

He nodded, kissed my cheek and went to the main hall, while I headed to Samaira's room.

I still can't believe my best friend is getting married.

Her love story had seen a lot of ups and downs. It's almost a miracle they are going to tie the knot today. From denying the feelings she had for Siddhant to crying like a lunatic for him, she had experienced every emotion in love.

I knocked and entered her room, to find her all ready in a beautiful traditional lehenga.

"Chahat, sweetheart, be with Samaira when she walks towards the hall," Samaira's mom said.

"Sure," I said.

I helped Samaira with her dress and together we walked to the wedding hall where Siddhant was waiting for her. I didn't miss the sudden happiness that filled his eyes when he first saw Samaira.

The rituals started and I went and stood next to Aryan. Throughout the ceremony, I saw different emotions in everybody's eyes. The happiness and content in Samaira and Siddhant's eyes and ecstasy along with a tint of sadness in her parents'.

By the time the rituals ended and Samaira and Siddhant were declared an official couple, even Samaira had tears in her eyes.

Bidding goodbyes is the hardest thing in life, especially when we are neither expecting it, nor prepared for it.

In Samaira's case, I was just not prepared for it. I may sound like her mom, but it was true. Attending your best friend's wedding is the best feeling ever, but saying goodbye to her is the worst.

"Chahat, I'll miss you," Samaira cried as she hugged me.

"Oh, I'll miss you too. You know I am just a call away. Make beautiful babies, you two, and be happy," I said, crying but trying to lighten up the situation at the same time.

She laughed and nodded. Then she sat in the car along with Siddhant and they went towards the airport. Samaira's family was still in tears and so was I.

"Chahat, let's go," Aryan said as he wiped my tears.

I nodded slightly and we went home. We changed and got into covers. Aryan came close to me like a cuddly bear. I smiled at his innocent ways.

I just wished to have this weirdo, moronic yet loveable and handsome man beside me. Always. It's wondrous how someone walks into your life in the form of an answer to your prayers and a meaning to your existence.

Aryan

The alarm buzzed next to me and that irked me.

"Chahat, please stop this alarm," I murmured in my sleep, but there was no response.

"Chahat!" I groaned, but again, there was no answer.

I knew Chahat was a light sleeper, and if she wasn't answering, she must be up to something. I opened my eyes, and much to my shock, there was no sign of Chahat. I got up and went to the washroom to check there, but there was no one there. Her dress from yesterday lay on the couch and above that was a note. I picked the note; it was from Chahat.

Hi Aryan!

There was an urgent call for me and that's why I left early. Don't have enough time to explain. I'll give you a call in the morning. Don't worry, I am fine.

Lots of love
Chahat.

"You could have woken me up!" I said out loud.

God knew what was so urgent that she couldn't wait a minute.

I checked my phone to make sure I hadn't missed any call from Chahat. Making sure of that, I got ready and called my driver.

Not being able to control myself, I called Chahat, but her number was not reachable. I messaged her that I have left her house and asked her to call me as soon as possible. I tried calling her again, but it was not reachable. I was getting nervous about the whole situation.

After reaching the office, I went straight to my floor and called up my trusted men.

"I want you all to leave your present work and track Chahat's mobile phone and find her. Go anywhere, I don't care, and all I care about is Chahat. Find her NOW!" I ordered and almost shouted at the end.

They immediately left my office and started looking for her. I sighed deeply and wondered where she could be.

I was unable to focus on anything except her.

'Is she safe?'

'Aryan, think positive,' my inner voice reminded.

'Yes, I have to think positive. She's safe. Nothing is going to harm her. She'll call me soon and I'll hear her melodious voice. I'll see her beautiful and angelic face again. After all, she can't stay away from teasing me.'

I sat back, closed my eyes and remembered the first time I had seen her. It was the last day of school after which we would be going to college. Everyone had changed their schools, but we three musketeers, Siddhant, Abhi and I were together like always.

Aryan

March 2006

"Siddhant, Abhi, that was insane," I said laughing post our prank.

"Seriously. The reaction of that boy was just so hilarious," Abhi said and laughed.

Just when I was about to speak, a person crashed with me, making her fall and me stumble.

"Oh sorry. I wasn't looking," I said as I regained my balance.

"Yeah of course! Idiots like you don't really look," the girl said rudely.

"Excuse me, I said sorry although it was equally your mistake. You could have changed your path," I said with equal amount of rudeness.

"Well, these books were blocking my view, I am sure I didn't see some moron coming my way," she said and that's when I saw books scattered on the floor.

"Well, your mistake. You should have thought about that before taking so many books," I said.

"Oh, believe me, I did. I thought that people with eyes would obviously see me and make way, but I just forgot that some morons without eyes also exist here," she said again, picked up her books and walked past us without looking back.

"Who is this hot tempered and super feisty girl?" I asked.

"Chahat Aggarwal. Wait, bro, you don't know? She was in the same grade," Abhi said.

"Oh! I don't really remember. Well, it doesn't really matter now, does it? School is over," I said.

"Yeah. How about celebrating the beginning of college?" Siddhant asked.

"Sure. Let's go, and Aryan, please walk carefully and not like a moron," Abhi said and both of them laughed.

"Whatever, dumb heads," I said, making them laugh more.

They walked ahead and then suddenly I turned towards the direction that little feisty girl had gone.

"Chahat Aggarwal." I muttered and smirked to myself.

∾

"Dude, I don't know about that. What about you?" I heard someone speak behind me, but I couldn't care less.

"Hello!" A hand waved in front of me, pulling me out of a daze.

"Oh... yeah. What's up?" I asked, clueless about what was happening around.

"You seem lost. Any problem?" Siddhant asked.

"No. I am fine. I was just thinking about something," I said.

"Oh! Something or someone?" Abhi teased.

"Shut up," I said taking my phone out of my pocket. I logged into my Facebook account and searched for the person who hadn't left my mind since we first met.

Chahat's profile opened and I couldn't help but gape at how beautiful she looked in her profile picture. I sent her a friend request without thinking.

I kept my phone aside and joined in the conversation. Getting tired of just hanging around, we decided to crash at my place. Abhi and Siddhant slept and just as I was about to close my eyes too, my phone beeped.

I lazily picked up my phone and was shocked to see that Chahat had accepted my friend request.

Did this just happen for real? Oh yes!

Calm your ass, Aryan, I reminded myself.

Should I message her? If yes, then what should I say?

'Hi?' No, *she'll think I am some kind of a creep.*

'Did you get hurt when you fell down?' That's so dumb. She'll think I am making fun of her.

'Hi, I am sorry about today.' Yes! That sounds great.

I immediately messaged her, but to my disappointment, she wasn't online.

I sighed and scrolled through my news feed to pass the time. The wait was killing me and I had no idea why.

I was about to give up and sleep, when my phone beeped, indicating a message from her.

A smile automatically came onto my face.

Chahat: *Hey! That's okay and even I am sorry, I was also a bit too rude.*

Aryan: *That's all right. So, you usually sleep this late?*

Chahat: *No, not this late. Actually, I was caught up with a painting.*

Oh! So, she paints. We talked for a while before we both called it a night. I kept my phone aside and smiled to myself. She surely was different, way too unique.

In a world full of people trying to copy each other, only a few unique people draw our attention, make us feel comfortable and capture our hearts.

Time passed and we gradually got close. She started to share every little detail related to her life with me, her new college and her friends and so did I. The more I talked to her, the more I realised that she was a big softie. She was very gentle and kind-hearted. She was the kind of girl who people consider to be almost extinct. She was the one who was always ready to help everyone, no matter what.

Some people become so important to us as if they are the oxygen that we take in, the water that quenches our thirst and everything that is vital for living.

And Chahat had reached that level of importance in my life.

The days we planned to go out were the days I looked forward to. The times she smiled were the most adored times for me. The moments when she held my hand were the moments I cherished. It was flabbergasting that someone who I didn't even know existed some time back, meant the world to me today.

I wanted to make her mine; she was everything I ever wanted, I have ever needed and she was just so special to me. All I wanted was to be with her and call her mine, but I had to make sure that I make her feel special, as she deserved to feel that.

I texted her to meet me that Sunday outside her college, and she agreed.

∾

Finally, it was Sunday. I reached her college and texted her, informing my arrival.

"Hey!" I heard a voice behind me and I instantly turned.

"Hey, little one," I said and looked at her.

"I am not little, tall man." She whined just like a five-year-old.

"Oh, you are. Come on, get inside the car," I said opening the door for her.

She made a face at me but got in anyway. I smiled at her.

"Let's put some rocking music. After all, this is such a beautiful evening," Chahat said as she played the radio.

Some 90's classics started to play and Chahat started singing along at the top of her lungs.

"I love this track. Come on Aryan, sing along. It's too much fun!" she said as she kept her hand on mine.

I started to sing along and by the time it ended, Chahat and I started laughing about how awful we were at singing.

We reached the place I had decided I would propose to her at and just then I could feel my heart picking up a fast rhythm. Suddenly my palms were getting sweaty and I was very nervous. A fear of how she would react started to hover on my mind.

I parked the car and stared at the entry of the park, the park which held the biggest surprise for Chahat. The park which would witness the start of our love story or the end of our friendship.

I felt a warm hand on my palm and I turned to see a worried Chahat.

"Are you okay, Aryan? You look pale. I'll get a water bottle for you," she said and was about to go when I held her arm and shook my head.

"No, Chahat, I am fine," I said. Only if she knew the real reason behind me being pale.

"Are you sure? Come on, let's go and take in some fresh air," she asked, to which I nodded and got out of the car. I took Chahat's hand in mine as we entered the park. For a moment I thought she would pull her hand back, but she didn't. She smiled at me that awakened a new feeling of hope in me. The hope of her saying yes, the hope of calling her mine.

"Why are we here?" Chahat asked, looking around.

"You don't like it?" I asked, looking at her.

"No! I love it! It's beautiful, so green, so lively and even the weather is really nice today. I asked because this isn't the kind of place where we mostly hang out. By the way, how can people not come here on such a lovely day? The place looks so deserted," she said.

"I am glad you liked it. Yes, it's surprising that there aren't many people around here," I said.

Well, luck was totally on our side, I guessed.

"You also have a thing for parks?" she asked, smiling.

"Well, yes. It's really nice to be here. I love how positive this place is!" I said.

"Hey, it's like I am listening to myself talk. I believe in the same. High five!" she said, excitedly.

I chuckled and high-fived her. She smiled and again placed her hand in mine.

Soon, we would reach the bridge, the place where I planned to propose to her. So, I requested Chahat to close her eyes. She looked at me in surprise, but agreed as I insisted. I moved forward with her hand in mine. The bridge was visible at a distance. I smiled internally because of how beautiful it looked with the lights and balloons. The decoration was just the way I liked and wanted it to be.

I moved to the centre of the bridge with Chahat standing opposite me and asked her to open her eyes. Chahat obliged and looked at the bridge with glowing eyes and an open mouth. I instantly knew she had liked it.

She smiled and twirled, admiring the place.

"It's beautiful, isn't it?" she asked, without moving an inch from where she was standing.

"Yes. Very beautiful, just like you," I said, looking into her eyes.

She blushed, looked down and murmured a small thank you.

I moved towards her and slowly put my hand under her chin to make her look at me.

I studied her face, she looked so beautiful with those pretty and big brown eyes. My eyes went down to her perfectly shaped nose and then to her perfect lips.

It was then that I realised it was the first time that we were standing this close to each other. Indeed, we had met a number of times before, spent quality time and got to know each other, but we never got this close.

After all those times, Chahat had found a best friend in me. I hadn't only found my best friend in her, but also my love.

I had begun to develop feelings for her. Feelings I had never experienced with anyone before. The feelings of true love, the feeling of becoming a better 'me', just for the sake of someone else.

I realised that a part of me was missing before and it was only after I met her that I felt complete.

I looked at her again and saw her looking at me intently.

'God! How much I love her!'

I got back into my senses and felt it was time to confess.

"Turn around, Chahat," I said softly.

She looked at me questioningly, before turning around and I saw how her eyes widened.

There were five little girls of the same height, wearing similar white frocks with matching hair bands and shoes, each holding a balloon with a word written on it.

Together they read:

'Will you be mine, Chahat?'

I slowly moved closer to her and whispered in her ear, "I love you, Chahat. I love you very much."

Chahat

I turned around and looked at him questioningly. 'Was I shocked?' Hell yes! I was beyond shocked.

My mind still trying to take in what had just happened!

I looked at those little girls who held balloons in their hands again.

I have seen a thousand proposals, but this was definitely the best! No kidding.

Suddenly, I felt someone's breath on my neck and I felt goosebumps. My heartbeat increased. My cheeks felt warm and my body was excited.

Gosh!

"I love you Chahat! I love you very much!" Aryan whispered in my ears.

I turned around looking at him in his eyes.

I opened my mouth to say something, but closed it, realising I had no words to say. I was speechless!

"Chahat, I know it's a bit sudden for you, I'll give you time, as much time as you want, but I just have one request. Please give it a thought. I am not a guy who randomly says 'I love you' to every possible girl. I have never even thought about any other girl from the moment you came into my life," he said.

"Aryan, I..." I started.

"No Chahat, I know it's hard for you to believe it, but I meant each and every word that I said. Our first meeting hadn't been the best, but it definitely drew me towards you. I wanted to know every single thing about you. From your mind to your heart and then your soul. I want to see that gorgeous and beautiful smile on your face, always. I love you, Chahat! I love you very, very much! Please give us a chance," he said and I found his eyes shining.

His words sounded so honest to me.

"Aryan, I respect your feelings, but I have always seen you as my best friend," I tried to explain, but it wasn't that. It was a certain fear I felt.

"Hey! I know! I half expected that answer. The good thing is that you didn't decline it. Chahat, I know it's difficult to imagine me like that after such a pure friendship, but please do give it a thought," he said.

"Of course, Aryan. I will." I said, not having anything else to say.

"Thank you so much, Chahat and yes, whatever your answer is, I will never stop loving you and will accept whatever you decide. After all, your happiness is what matters to me more than anything else," he said, smiling.

I smiled brightly at him and nodded. He took my hand in his and guided me to the back of the garden to a beautiful table arranged for two.

My favourite food was already kept there. Well, by food I mean PIZZA!

We had a heartful of pizza and after that the dessert was chocolate cake! Everything was of my choice and I was actually surprised and happy that Aryan knew every little detail about me and kept it in mind while planning about today.

Today was indeed really special, and the credit for that goes to Aryan.

After that, we got into the car and drove back to where he had picked me from.

"Thank you so very much Aryan! Today was really special and I am so happy that you put so much effort just to make it memorable for both of us!" I said after getting out of the car.

"Hey! That's my duty, after all. Your smile is my responsibility, Chahat! Your smile lights up my day, so get ready… I'm going to do anything for this beautiful curve on your face," he said.

My heart swelled at that and I couldn't help but give him a tight hug. It was the first time when my heart skipped a beat and I felt warm. I smiled at him as I pulled away and waved at him before getting back to my campus.

Time flew since Aryan proposed to me and I would be lying if I said I wasn't attracted towards him. Every day, I woke up to a really cute and positive good morning text that made me feel special. He cared about me a lot and never lacked in depicting his love for me. He was way too motivating, cheerful, positive, focused and loveable.

My best friend, Samaira, who was studying in London, also knew about Aryan and was advising me to say yes to him and giving it a try, and if it hadn't been for my fear, I would have said yes to Aryan that day itself.

"Hey Chahat!" Someone said from behind me as I was walking towards my hostel in the college campus.

I turned to find my dearest roommate, Reeya.

"Hey Reeya. How was your day?" I asked.

"It was good. How was yours?" she said.

"It was great. So, what's up?" I asked.

"Well, I am really, really tired from all the classes and the assignments they keep giving us every day." She whined like a baby.

"Oh! Well, I guess that makes two of us . So, are you free or have some work?" I asked.

"Well, I am free today! What about you?" She asked.

"I also am free. How about we spend the day lazing around and watching Netflix?" I asked.

"That would be amazing," she said, happily.

I smiled and we went to our room. As I was about to go inside the room, I saw a bouquet of flowers outside the door. It had flowers of different colours and it looking nothing less than beautiful!

I spotted a note along with it and some of my favourite chocolates.

I picked it all up and went inside the room. I kept the flowers and chocolates on the bed before opening the note that was inside an envelope.

Hey beautiful!

I hope you had a great and productive day at college. This is to make you smile and lighten up your day. Also, it's just a small reminder of how much I love you.

With love,
Aryan.

I smiled at such a sweet gesture by Aryan and immediately messaged him of how much I loved the flowers and thanked him for such a sweet surprise.

"Aww! Aryan is such a cutie! I really wish I had a lover like him," I heard Reeya say beside me.

"Reeya, Aryan is my best friend, not a lover. He just likes me, so yeah..." I said as I started putting the flowers in a vase.

"More like he loves you," she said as she made herself comfortable on her bed.

"Maybe," I said as I was done putting the flowers away with the chocolates and the note secured at a side.

"So, what's the problem? I still don't get it," she asked.

"As in?" I asked confusingly as I got comfortable on my bed.

"As in, why haven't you accepted his proposal? I mean he had proposed to you in an amazing manner. I still don't understand why you haven't said 'yes' yet," she said.

"Yes, I get that he has proposed to me really nicely, but the thing is, I don't know whether it's too early or is it fine," I said.

"Finally, Chahat speaks about this! What do you mean?" she asked, sitting up.

"I mean, I want to start a relationship with Aryan. He's amazing. He's like my definition of perfect and he's everything I want. It's just that I have always heard relationships don't last long and the spark, too, ends and I dread it. I have never been in any relationship before and I am scared of getting my heart broken in the end," I said as I finally let it out.

"Chahat, I understand, and believe me, everybody feels the same. Nobody wants to get their heart broken. No relationship is all sunshine and rainbows, but people still have relationships. They still fall in love, knowing it can result in sleepless nights and infinite tears. It's just that people find the ones who are worth it," she said.

"How?" I asked.

"They don't look for someone who suits their status or standards. They look for someone who is willing to love them and accept them. They look for someone with whom they won't mind spending the rest of their life. Even if you are scared to start a relationship, just look for someone you really can't do without and before that, just think whether getting your heart broken by him will be worth it or not. After all, it's not always that you'll have to break up. Maybe you can live the term 'forever' with him," she said.

"Maybe," I said.

"So, can you do without Aryan?" she asked.

"I don't know, but yes, I am afraid to lose him. He's someone who knows my heart, he knows all of my flaws, but he still makes me feel so beautiful and special," I said.

"Okay, so imagine, one day Aryan decides to move on with someone else. How are you going to react?" she asked.

Aryan with someone else?

The thought immediately ignited pain in my heart. I can't even imagine Aryan with someone else, holding her hand, walking with her, kissing her, calling her cute names. I can't.

"I got the answer," she said with a smirk.

"Huh?" I asked.

"Missy, your facial expression screams jealousy," she said.

"Does it?" I asked.

"Yes. Chahat, you know what? You love him as well. You are just so dumb that you needed someone to knock some sense into you. So go tell him what you feel before it's too late," she said.

I recalled her words and just then my phone buzzed with his reply.

Anything for you, Chahat and no thank yous. You deserve all the happiness and I'll make sure you get it.

I guess it's time.

Aryan

"Well, I guess he's totally whipped," I heard Siddhant speak beside me.

"Who?" I ask.

"Abhi," he said.

"What makes you say that all of a sudden?" I asked sipping my cold coffee in the canteen of the college.

"Well, look straight ahead of you and you'll know," he said sipping his green apple mojito.

I looked and found Abhi talking to Kaira, our classmate from school.

"I couldn't agree more," I said, smirking.

After that, Abhi came to our table and sat down on the chair opposite to ours.

"What's up?" he said.

"Someone's head over heels in love with Kaira," Siddhant said.

"Oh well," Abhi said rubbing the back of his neck.

I laughed and just then my phone buzzed. I picked it up and saw a message from a WhatsApp group chat but also saw a message from Chahat from earlier, which I must have missed.

I immediately opened it.

Thank you so much for the flowers! I loved them. Specially the note and the chocolates. You definitely know how to brighten my day and mood.

I smiled, knowing she liked the little surprise I had planned for her.

I texted back and then looked up and saw those two idiots looking at me.

"Sid, you were talking about me being in love. Look! We have got one more right here," Abhi said, smirking.

"I know, right!" Siddhant said.

"Shut up guys!" I said.

"Hasn't she said 'yes' yet?" Sid said.

"Nope, but I won't give up," I said, smiling.

"Aryan, you know you can have anyone you want. So why are you still after her, knowing that she is just making you wait?" Sid asked.

"Well, she's the one I really love and I am ready to do anything for her. If that means waiting, then I am ready to wait," I said.

"God, both my boys are whipped!" Siddhant said and we both laughed.

Just then, my phone buzzed with a text from Chahat.

Chahat: *Are you free? Can you meet me in the same park where we had gone that day?*

Aryan: *Sure. I am on my way, but what happened? Anything serious?*

Chahat: *Everything's fine. Don't worry. Drive safe.*

I hurried to the park and reached there after almost an hour. Well, thanks to the traffic.

I texted Chahat that I had arrived and she directed me to the bridge. I moved towards the bridge and as I walked, my heart was beating faster. What could it be?

I saw her standing there already, facing the other side. She was wearing a beautiful sundress with her hair open, just the way I liked.

"Chahat," I called as I took a step on the bridge.

She slowly turned towards me with a beautiful smile on her face.

"Aryan," she started, "Would like to tell you that I love you and will you be my boyfriend?" She said the words so quickly that I couldn't understand anything.

"What?" I sounded confused. "Hey! Why are you so nervous? Say it slowly." I said, going close to her and holding her hands in mine.

She took a deep breath.

"Aryan, I am saying that I am sorry I couldn't organise an amazing proposal plan like yours, but I wanted to tell you that I really love you. Will you be mine?" She asked, turning red.

I was dumbstruck at her confession and blinked my eyes to make sure she had actually said it.

I looked at Chahat again, looking at me nervously.

I smiled a big grin or probably the biggest grin that was possible and I almost shouted, "I love you too, Chahat!"

She smiled happily and in an instant, she left my hands and put her arms around my neck and hugged me tightly.

I was taken aback, but soon I recovered and hugged her back, as tightly I could. I held her close to me and it was definitely one of the best feelings ever!

Chahat

I looked at him nervously as he held my hands. I just loved how my hands fit in his.

He was shocked at first, but then, suddenly his shocked face broke into a big smile and he almost shouted the words, "I love you too, Chahat."

I don't know what got into me as I instantly kind of threw myself on him and wrapped my arms around him. I hugged him as tightly as I could, with a big smile on my face. It felt like heaven when he held me in his arms. It made me feel like I was safe. It felt as though nothing could go wrong when he held me like that.

My inner voice told me to hold onto this guy and I did just that. My fast pounding heart told me that my decision wasn't wrong. Aryan was making me experience the kind of things I had never felt before and I would be honest to say that I was loving that a lot. That moment was so beautiful that if I were told to spend my entire life like that, I would have happily agreed.

"You have no idea how happy you've made me!" he said.

I smiled at him and held his hands in mine.

"And I can't describe how lucky I feel to have you in my life. You make my life so much better," I said, looking right into his eyes.

"I am glad I could do that, but what happened suddenly? If it was my flowers that made you say 'yes', then believe me, baby, I would do that over and over," he said.

I laughed to that and my heart swelled when he used the term of endearment to call me.

"Well, my roommate just knocked some sense into me. I realised that my happiness lies with you and I was ready to give us a chance. So, I planned to call you here and propose. I really wanted it to be special, just like the way you did, but I was short of time and couldn't come up with anything creative," I said.

"Well, in that case, remind me to thank her. Chahat, believe me that I plan to give you that happiness all life long, and I'll work hard with as much love and focus as I can, to always make you feel loved, happy and cared for. You'll never have to regret giving us a chance, Chahat!" He said.

"God! You are going to make me cry now," I said while blushing a bit.

He laughed at that and after that, we decided to walk around and talk. Whenever we were together, I always felt happy, but this time, there was something more – I also felt loved.

Was it the change that our relationship had brought?

I looked at the guy beside me who was smiling as he talked. To be honest, he had the most beautiful smile ever.

"You have a beautiful smile," I blurted out all of a sudden and it took me a moment to realise what I had just said out loud.

"Oh, thank you!" he said, smiling more but I also spotted his cheeks turning a bit red.

"Oh my god! Did Aryan Kapoor just blush?" I said, laughing.

"Shut up! I did not," he said, rolling his eyes.

"You did," I said and he rolled his eyes with a smile.

We then decided to go back and, on the way, Bollywood hits were playing on the radio as we both sat silently. But it wasn't some awkward silence, it was a comfortable silence as Aryan held my hand while driving and I smiled at it.

It's small moments like these that leave the most beautiful imprints in our hearts.

Soon we reached my college and I was about to get out of the car when he stopped me and opened the door for me.

"You know I could've done that myself," I said as I got out of the car.

"What type of a gentleman would I be if I let my girl open the door?" he said.

My heart swelled yet again when he called me his girl.

Is it just me or does everyone find it cute to be called 'my girl' from the person they love?

I blushed and said a small 'thank you'. As I moved a step past him, I turned towards him and gave him a tight hug before whispering a small 'bye' in his ear. I then moved to the college with a big smile on my face.

Our relationship grew stronger with each passing day. Aryan proved to be the best boyfriend in the entire world. Not only did he pamper me, he also helped me grow more mature and strong. With him in my life, there were never any dull moments and I never felt alone or sad. He told me how much he loved me, how blessed he was to have me and how special I was to him, every day. He was an actual blessing in my life!

"Hey angel!" Someone whispered in my ear from behind and kissed my cheek as I sat on a chair in the college's library.

I turned to see Aryan as he made himself comfortable on the chair next to me.

"Aryan! What are you doing here?" I asked keeping the novel that was in my hand, on the table in front of me.

"Miss Chahat, it would be really nice of you if you maintain the decorum of the library," the librarian said.

I mouthed a 'sorry' to the librarian and the rest of the students who were glaring at me and turned back to Aryan.

"What are you doing here?" I whispered this time.

"Well, I sneaked here to surprise you," he said, smiling.

Did I mention that I had been getting such cute surprises for the past three months?

"But how did they let you in?" I asked, confused.

"I have my ways." He said, winking at me.

"Oh!" That was all I could say.

"Yeah," he said as he held my hand and played with my fingers.

"Chahat?" He said after five minutes of silence and me going back to reading.

"Hmm?" I hummed.

"You know, I was thinking whether you'd like to come with me to a place this Saturday night," He said.

"Where?" I asked, looking at him.

"There's a nice place I know and I'll not tell you where, but believe me, you'll love it. Just say yes, please," he said.

"That means tomorrow night?" I asked.

"Yes, since you spend the weekends at home, so why not go then?" he said.

"I guess I'll have to sneak out. Anyhow, I'll tell you," I said.

"Okay," he said smiling.

After college, I went back home. My house was in Mumbai, and I only lived in the hostel to enjoy the hostel life, if you know what I mean.

"Hey mom," I said as I entered the living room and hugged her.

"Hi Chahat. How are you? How're Reeya and Samaira?" she asked.

"I am good and they are good as well. How are you and dad?" I asked.

"We both are doing great. That reminds me, your dad and I are leaving for London tomorrow morning," she said.

"You always tell me about every important thing so soon," I said sarcastically.

"Well, I told you this now because I was sure that my little girl would have already forgotten that I had told the same thing to her two weeks back," she said.

Oops.

"Oh...well, I remembered that. I was just kidding around, you know," I said, trying to cover it up.

"Of course," she said sarcastically and smiled sweetly.

My mom is one in a million, I swear!

I sat down beside her and texted Aryan.

Chahat: *Mom and dad are leaving for London tomorrow.*

Aryan: *The plan's on then?*

Chahat: *Yes.*

Aryan: *Oh great! See you soon, baby.*

I smiled. It had been three months already, but I was still not over his nicknames for me.

"What's his name?" suddenly Mom asked.

"Whose?" I asked, though I guess I had an idea of who she was referring to.

"Don't make me say it out loud. What's his name?" she asked.

"Whose, Mom? I don't know," I tried again.

"Chahat," She said.

I huffed and realised there was no escape.

"Aryan," I said.

"Oh. How long?" She said, surprisingly cool and all interested.

"Three months," I said.

"What does he do?" She asked.

"He's still studying," I said. "How did you know?" I added.

"Well, I have sources," she said, shrugging.

"Mom, please," I said.

"Well, you were smiling while looking at your phone. So, I just tried and was about to give up... when you told me the name yourself," she said, trying to control her laugh.

My eyes widened to that, making her laugh harder.

"This is not fair!" I whined and went to my room.

Mom and dad left for London the next morning and after that, I just killed time, goofing around.

"Where's he?" I wondered out loud, when it started to get dark outside and there was no call or text from him.

I sighed and locked the main door and all the windows before walking to my room.

I browsed a bit on TV and finally settled on watching a movie. After some time, the bell rang. I got up, switched off the television and went down. I opened the door and saw Aryan standing there.

"Where have you been?" I asked as he hugged me and kissed my cheek.

"You look cuddly," he said as he nuzzled his nose on my neck.

He loved doing that!

"But where have you been?" I asked again, realising he didn't reply earlier.

"I was busy with implementing your surprise," he said.

I nodded to that as he pulled away.

"Switch off all the lights and lock the door," he said and after 5 minutes, we were in his car.

"So, where are we going?" I asked him as we drove off.

"Well, that's for me to know and you to find out," he said, winking.

"Oh, come on! Tell me!" I whined like a kid.

"Chahat, you'll find out soon," he said.

I huffed and sat back. I saw us driving away from the city and up somewhere which seemed to me like a hill. I was looking around and realised I had never been in this part of city. Just then, I felt the car coming to a halt. Aryan got out, came to my side and opened the door for me.

"So, here we are," he said.

"Why are we here?" I asked.

"Well, this place has been my childhood escape. Whenever I needed time to myself, I used to sneak out of home and come here." He said sighing.

"Oh," was all I could say.

"Come," he said, holding my hand.

We came to the end point which had a railing and from there

I could see the lights of the city sparkling beautifully. The sight was totally breath-taking and amazing. The wind was blowing softly, but powerfully enough to free my hair from behind my ear. I felt like I was flying; I felt like I was in heaven.

"Chahat, isn't it beautiful?" Aryan asked.

"Yes. It's amazing," I said, still amazed at the sight in front of me.

He then guided me to a side and as much as I wanted to stay there and look at that amazing sight, I went along. I spotted a double mattress laid on the ground with pillows and a blanket. There was also a basket kept on the side. We slowly lay down on that mattress and I looked at the diamond-like stars shining up in the sky.

I was hypnotised, lost in their beauty.

"Chahat, you know your eyes shine better than those stars in the sky," Aryan said suddenly, playing with my fingers.

"I wish it was the truth," I said, chuckling.

"It is. Maybe it's hard for you to believe, but on a serious note, your eyes have a better shine than those stars," he said.

"Oh really, Mr Kapoor?" I asked, turning towards him.

"Oh yes, Ms Aggarwal," he said, turning towards me.

I looked into his eyes and felt that today was somewhat different. He had planned such a surprise for me like always, but this time he made me feel more special, because he got me to a place which was a part of his childhood, which was a part of him.

It made me feel like he was ready to show me his raw self, his deepest, darkest self.

"Chahat, what are you thinking?" he said, looking at me.

"Just how handsome you are," I said, kissing his nose. Well, that was half true!

"Says the most beautiful girl," he said.

"Lol," I said, smiling.

"What? You are the most beautiful and the prettiest girl inside out. I swear, I thank god each day that he has blessed me with a girl like you," he said, looking deep into my eyes.

My heart swelled at that and all I wanted was to take him in my arms and kiss him and pour all my love into him, but I controlled myself. I took his hand in mine instead.

"I love you," I blurted out, my cheeks turning a deep shade of red.

Aryan looked at me before his thin lips broke in a wide grin.

"I love you more than words could ever explain, Chahat. You are my world," he said.

I smiled as we slowly moved closer to each other until our lips met.

Suddenly, all things around me disappeared. Nothing else seemed to matter other than Aryan's lips on mine. He was kissing me softly; it was so soft that I could literally melt by the softness of it.

He kissed me with all his love and slowly I started to return his kiss, pouring all the love I felt for him into the kiss.

I was in another world, a world that knew no separation, no partition. A world which knew nothing but love and love alone.

Thousands of butterflies fluttered around in my stomach, my heart's pace was increasing as every second passed and I could feel goosebumps on my skin.

My hands found their way to his hair as his hands went around my waist. I shuddered in his arms as we continued to lie down and kiss. I could feel him smile against my lips and I couldn't help but smile too.

Slowly, we pulled away and I stared in his eyes to find them sparkling under the night sky. He looked back at me and I knew he was trying to find some reaction on my face.

To relieve his tension, I smiled brightly at him and buried my face in the crook of his neck. I could feel that he had let out a sigh of relief before wrapping his arms around me and I had never felt that safe before.

We stayed like that for a few minutes before I pulled away and looked at him. He looked down at me and I slowly moved closer to him and pecked his lips.

"I love you," I whispered.

"I love you more, Chahat. You are all I want and all I would ever need," Aryan said, while kissing my forehead. We then got up and started to eat.

"So Chahat, tell me something about the life you want afterwards," he said, taking a bite of his sandwich.

"I just want to live a normal life. Nothing like a stunning life but a simple life which makes me happy. I can't have a 9 to 5 job, I want to do something that makes me feel alive. I'll nearly be a dead soul if I found myself doing some routine work everyday," I said honestly.

"And if I'm not wrong, you feel painting makes you feel alive?" he asked.

"Absolutely. It helps me de-stress and just, you know, shut the world out. I am myself and I am happy, but how do you know?" I said, smiling.

"Amazing! In a world where everyone is running after money, I am glad my girl is the one who looks for happiness," he said, smiling.

I blushed.

"Thank you, but you haven't answered me. How do you know?" I asked.

"Well, I know you well enough to know that your escape is painting," he replied.

"Okay, so your turn. Tell me one of your fears," I said, taking a bite of my pasta.

"Losing you," he said, looking deep into my eyes.

"Honestly, please?" I added, smiling.

"Honestly. From the day you have entered in my life, my life makes sense. I never thought I would get a girl like you. I often asked myself 'will I ever get a girl who will make those cheesy love stories seem like a reality? Will love ever happen to me?' But my question was answered when I met you. I was attracted to you from the first instance. I didn't know I had it in me," he said.

"Had what?" I asked.

"Like planning dates, planning small surprises, finding ways to see my girl smile. You make me believe in love, Chahat. I know it's too early to say this, but I really want to marry you because you are an amazing girl! I don't even think I could function properly if you leave me one day. I'll die..." I cut him off by hugging him as tightly as I could.

"I love you, Aryan." I said while hugging him and pulled away from him only to shower kisses on his face.

"I love you more, little one," he said, smiling while looking at me intently.

I laughed at the name and slowly moved my fingers on his face. His eyes closed at the instant my fingers made contact with his forehead. I slowly moved my fingers on his forehead before moving down to his eyes and then to his perfectly shaped nose and then to his lips. His lips parted beneath my touch. His lips were so soft, and suddenly he opened his beautiful eyes.

He kissed my thumb that was tracing his lips. I moved my

hand from there while we both looked in each other's eyes and moved to his cheeks, his beard slightly poking my fingers.

I smiled at him and pinched both of his cheeks and he smiled.

"You look very cute like that," I said, laughing.

"Wait," I said and took out my phone and took his photo with him smiling and my hand pinching his cheek.

"This is one of my favourites," I said, laughing while I was looking at that picture.

After spending some time under the stars, he dropped me home at around 2:00 a.m. I couldn't help but smile to myself and feel extremely blessed to have Aryan in my life.

∾

You don't know how time flies by when you are deeply in love. That year had probably been the best year of my life. Aryan was focused on our relationship with as much love, focus and care that he puts in his work!

He had been among the top students of his class and so was I among my English honour classes.

Holding hands and kissing each other was normal for us both. He usually showered me with his sweet gestures and I, too, made sure to do the same for him. I could laugh like a lunatic, but still be sure he would accept me. I could act at my worst, but still be sure he would find me the best. I could be the ugliest person, but still be sure he would find me the most beautiful.

That day, we had planned to meet his best friends, Siddhant and Abhi. My close friend and Abhi's girlfriend Kaira was also coming along. It's been quite a while since I met her and I was so excited!

Well, Siddhant was still single and he became a good friend of mine (all thanks to Aryan). I really didn't know how Samaira would feel about that, considering she had a crush on Siddhant from school days.

I put on my watch before picking up my bag and left after saying bye to mom.

I saw Aryan's car at the corner and sat in the passenger seat.

"Hello, pretty girl. How did I get so lucky to have such a beauty like you sitting in the passenger seat of my car?" he said the moment I sat and got comfortable.

"Well, I guess my boyfriend won't be happy if he finds me sitting here with you," I said, pretending to check my nails.

"Oh, don't worry, pretty girl! You're safe with me. We won't tell your boyfriend," he said in a hushed voice as if telling a secret. I laughed to that but stopped when I saw him staring at me.

"What?" I asked, smiling.

"Are you a magician?" he asked suddenly.

"What? Why?" I asked, clearly confused.

"Because whenever I look at you, everything around me seems to fade away," he said.

"Did you just use a cheesy pick up line on me?" I asked and laughed hard.

"I am glad my search on pickup lines was worth my time because that made you laugh," he said, smiling. I laughed harder on that.

"What?" he asked, smiling.

"Who searches for pickup lines on the internet?" I said.

"Well, I do, and it was worth it because it made my girl laugh," he said, while starting the engine of the car. I shook my head and soon, we reached the mall. After parking, he came to my side and took my hand in his before walking inside the mall. We met everyone, and Kaira and I hugged each other tightly.

"I missed you!" I said to her.

"Me too! It's a shame that despite being in the same city we don't meet each other," she said.

"I totally agree! We have to work on that. How's Diya?" I asked. Diya was a part of our gang of four.

"Amazing. How's Samaira? I haven't met her either," she said.

"She's great as ever. We, too, catch up on video calls. She hardly comes back to India," I said.

"Come on! Let's go now," Aryan said and we had a great day at the mall.

∾

"Chahat, congratulations! Your assignment is the best and my personal favourite!" Our teacher, Mrs Rosie said.

"Thank you, Mrs Rosie," I said with a smile.

She nodded and dispersed the class. My phone buzzed while I was leaving for my home.

Aryan: *Hey! It's the weekend. So, are you free tonight?*

Chahat: *Yes, I am free, but I can't sneak out like last time.*

Aryan: *There's no need to sneak out. I'll talk to your mom. It's only for a dinner.*

Chahat: *How?*

Aryan: *Missy, there's a thing called Facebook. We connected there and let's just say your mom was quite happy to know about me.*

Chahat: *Oh! That's new. Anyways, where is the dinner?*

Aryan: *I'll tell you that later.*

Chahat: *No, tell me now. I have to pick a dress accordingly.*

Aryan: *Love, I'll tell you that and as far as your dress is concerned, keep it normal. Not too casual, not too formal.*

If only he knew how difficult it was to pick up a dress according to the description he gave me. I just shrugged it and after reaching home, started looking for a dress. I found the perfect attire and got ready before calling Aryan and telling him that I was ready. I walked downstairs to find Aryan already sitting there.

"Tall man, you already here!" I said as I walked towards him. He got up and side hugged me.

"My little one is stating the obvious yet again." He chuckled and I smacked his arm.

"You look beautiful, by the way," He added.

"Thank you! You don't look too bad yourself," I said.

"Young love," Mom said from behind.

After about thirty minutes, Aryan and I left my place. Also, it was incredible to even think that Aryan and mom were getting along exceptionally.

"Aryan, where are we going?" I asked.

"I'll tell you that when we are there. Till then relax, love," He said.

After sitting patiently and using my phone for about thirty minutes, I asked him again.

"Well, I guess now is the perfect time to tell you. We are going to have dinner at my place with my parents," he said casually.

"Oka- What?" I said, loudly. My eyes widened and my face almost lost its colour.

"Calm down, love! I didn't tell them to call you over for dinner. It was them! They love you and wanted me to invite you over. Believe me, there's nothing to freak out about, baby!" He said, rubbing my hand with his.

"Aryan, it's easy for you to say that," I said, sighing.

"Believe me, there's nothing to worry about. Look, we are here," he said.

My heart's pace increased on hearing that and I got more anxious than I already was.

As we entered, my eyes widened on seeing a big, white mansion. There was a beautiful garden in front of the mansion and a fountain placed in the centre. On the side I could see a few really expensive cars parked.

I was still admiring the place when Aryan stopped in front of the gate and got out of the car. A man came and took the car to park it.

"You should have waited. I was coming to open your door," Aryan said, taking my hand in his.

"I'm sorry. I was so stressed about this whole thing and was busy in admiring the place that I completely forgot," I admitted.

"I am glad you liked it, and Chahat, there's no need to worry. Come," he said and we walked to the main door of the house.

Just as Aryan was about to ring the door bell, the door opened and a woman came out, whom I assumed was Aryan's mother.

In an instant, Aryan's mother hugged me tightly and after coming out of the shock, I hugged her back.

"I'm so glad you came. You are more beautiful in reality than you look in your pictures!" She remarked and I smiled brightly. My nerves started to calm down.

"You, too, are really beautiful and no one could guess that you are a mom to a college going guy," I said, honestly. She was beautiful and looked younger than she actually was.

"Oh, thank you darling! Come in," she said and we walked inside.

The interior was more beautiful than the exterior of the place. Despite being very finely furnished and decorated, the place had a homely touch too that didn't make a person feel out of place.

"Oh! Look who's here! The one Aryan can't stop talking about," a voice came from behind and I guessed it was Aryan's dad.

"Hello uncle," I said, smiling.

"Hello dear! Come, sit! I am Aryan's dad," he said.

I took a seat and we all started to talk. And after a while, dinner was served.

I was extremely grateful that Aryan's parents liked me. They were kind-hearted and down to earth. Another thing that I learnt was to always meet Aryan's parents with an empty stomach, because they loved to make people eat!

∾

Such was the power of Aryan's love that I didn't realise how days turned into months and months into years. Three years had passed since I met him for the first time. Aryan's mom had become very fond of me and she was very excited about our graduation.

"Tell me about your plans for graduation," Aunty said, as she sat opposite Aryan and me, after we came back from college.

"Mine is on 30th of next month," Aryan said.

"And mine is on—" I started but Aryan has cut me off in between.

"On 28th of next month, I know," he said, sitting down.

"Stalker," I mouthed to him.

"Your stalker," he mouthed back, passing his boyish grin, to which I smiled.

"I'll call designers for you both. Get your dresses ready! It's already the end of this month," she said.

"You are talking as if you are talking about their wedding, honey," Aryan's dad spoke from behind. "Hey champs! Hey honey!" He continued while coming. He then sat on one of the sofas.

"Maybe, but I will be more excited about their wedding than I am right now," she said, laughing.

"That's true. Now I am starving! Let's go and eat something," he said.

"Sure. I'll just tell the maids to set up the table with snacks," aunty said while getting up.

"Great. Come Chahat, come Aryan," uncle said.

"Oh no, Uncle. I have to go home now. It's already 6," I said, taking up my handbag.

It wasn't the easiest to convince them to allow me to leave, but after they all agreed, I went to my car and drove back home.

"Hey mum. Hey dad," I greeted them as I entered home.

"Hey dear! How are you?" Dad asked.

"I'm great! You?" I asked.

"I am great too! So finally, my little one is graduating! Still can't believe that," he said.

"I know. Three years passed by really quick," I replied, sitting.

"Right. So, what's the plan for future?" Mom asked.

"Masters in the same field and I like teaching so maybe after that I'll take up the profession of teaching or something like a blogger," I replied.

"And Aryan?" Mom asked.

"He's doing MBA after graduation and then taking over his dad's company," I replied.

"Amazing. He's really smart," Mom said.

"Yes. He does sound smart to me, too. Anyway, let's have dinner now," Dad said. And after dinner, I went back to my room and I got a call from Samaira.

"Hey babe. What's up?" I asked.

"Just wrapped up in my blanket. Too cold, you see," she said.

"Right, but you must have adapted to it. You have been there for five years already," I said.

"Kind of. Anyway, what's wrong?" she asked, sensing my behaviour.

"I miss you girl! When are you coming back?" I asked, missing my best friend suddenly.

"Hey! I miss you too and I'll be there for a few weeks after my graduation," she replied.

"Just for a few weeks? You are coming back after like two years!" I said.

"As much as I love being in India, I have to be back early for preparation for my master's," she replied.

"I understand! Just be here, soon! Okay?" I said lovingly.

"Okay!" She said and I could sense a smile on her face.

Chahat

March 2009

Soon, it was my graduation day. I got dressed in my blue dress that reached just above my knees with a pair of heels.

Just as I turned, someone hugged me suddenly. I took a moment to realise what happened, when I heard 'surprise' and I knew that voice too well!

Samaira.

"Oh my god! Samaira!" I said and hugged her back, tightly.

"What's up, Chahat!" she said, once she had pulled away.

"I still can't believe you came! You were supposed to come next week," I said.

"Well, I did, but Aryan wanted to give you a surprise on your graduation day, so he called me and we planned it," Samaira said.

"Where is he? I haven't seen him yet! He told me he'll be here in the morning itself," I said.

"Right here, beautiful," Aryan said, entering the room with a beautiful bouquet.

"So sweet! Thank you, Aryan!" I said, trying to take the bouquet.

"Aye! Later, baby," he said, keeping it away.

I scoffed at him and he mimicked me before giving me the bouquet. I hugged him and kissed his cheek before turning towards Samaira.

"I came here directly from the airport," she said, yawning.

"Jet lagged?" I asked.

"Kind of, but don't worry. Let's get you to your college for your graduation!" she said, all excited.

"Okay then. Let's go!" Aryan said.

"Yes! Just let me freshen up a bit," Samaira said, making her way to the washroom.

"Congratulations, beautiful," Aryan said, coming near me.

"Thank you, handsome," I said, wrapping my arms around him while my other hand held the bouquet.

He kissed my forehead and my nose as he held me by my waist. Just as he was about to kiss me on my lips, we heard the door to my washroom opening and I pushed Aryan away.

"Oops. Sorry! Am I disturbing something?" Samaira asked.

"No, no! Let's go!" I said, looking at myself through the mirror.

After that, we went downstairs, and from there, to my college, along with my parents.

After my graduation ceremony was over, all of us had lunch together. Aryan and dad were getting along really great.

"Chahat, this is from your mom and me as a gift on your graduation!" Dad said.

"Thanks Mom and Dad!" I said and opened it to find a beautiful bracelet inside.

"It's gorgeous! I love you both," I said, smiling and putting it on my wrist.

"My turn! This is for you, Chahat. Congratulations!" Samaira said, giving me a box.

I opened it to find a super amazing art kit which I always wanted. It had every colour one could imagine and I was planning to get it on my birthday, but my best friend had already got it for me.

"Oh my! Thank you so much. You always know what to get for me," I said, smiling.

"And Chahat, this is from Mom and Dad. Since they are not home, they told me to give this to you," Aryan said placing a wrapped gift in front of me.

I opened it and found a beautiful long dress inside.

"This is so pretty! Say my thanks to uncle and aunty." I gasped.

"I am glad you liked it and you'll be getting my gift soon," Aryan said and winked.

Dad coughed and we got back.

"Thank you so much! I love you all," I said.

After lunch, Samaira went home. Aryan asked Mom and Dad, if he could take me with him and both of them said yes.

I didn't realise but I slept all my way to the place Aryan was taking me to and the next thing I remember was Aryan waking me up.

"Have we reached?" I asked.

"Yup," he said and helped me get off the car with those heels on.

"These heels are killing me," I muttered.

"Don't worry. Come," he said as he held my hand and I saw a beach which was completely empty.

It was decorated with beautiful lights and a table for two.

"Wow," I said.

He took my hand again and guided me to the table and made me sit on the chair. He sat down on his knees in front of me and began taking off my heels.

"Aryan! I can do that," I said, pulling my feet away.

"Allow me," he said, to which I sighed and then allowed him. He took off my heels and massaged my feet as if he was trying to remove the pain.

We walked towards the shore and I felt the water coming under my feet. It was the best feeling along with my hair flying away from behind my ears and moving along with the wind.

I turned towards Aryan and he was already looking at me. I smiled at him and the moment had a spark that made us move towards each other. Just a second later, we were in each other's arms, standing in the water and kissing each other passionately with all our love. We kissed and didn't stop. Running out of breath didn't matter anymore, because for now we were each other's oxygen, and maybe we forever will be.

There was a battle between our tongues and our lips, but the battle wasn't of hate or despair, but rather of love. We were kissing as if there was no tomorrow, as if it was our last kiss and I knew how I prayed that god continues to keep Aryan in my life.

After we finally pulled away, I smiled and held my hand out to him, as if asking him to hold it.

He smiled widely before holding my hand and giving it a squeeze of assurance that he was going to be with me forever. I squeezed his hand to assure him that I, too, was going to stay with him forever.

Our lips never said anything, but it was our eyes that spoke to each other along with our souls.

He's the one I have been looking for all my life. He's the one I have always dreamed of. He's a blessing. He's my angel. He's like a gift to me from god whom I am going to cherish. He completes me!

"Aryan, you are such a pure person and I am going to keep your life pure, even if I have to leave you. I promise," I said.

"Chahat, what do you mean?" Aryan asked shockingly.

"Aryan, I hate cruelty, criminals and killers. I can't tolerate hurting someone. I have not told you this, but I had a younger brother who was killed at the age of 7," I said with tears in my eyes.

Aryan hugged me tightly.

"Chahat, tell me what happened?" Aryan asked with concern.

"He was kidnapped by some criminals who asked for a hefty ransom in return. Dad agreed and arranged the amount to be paid. Somehow the police got involved although dad never informed them. The kidnappers killed my brother before escaping," I said, crying loudly.

"Oh my god! It's really very sad. I am so sorry, Chahat," Aryan said hugging me tightly and wiping my tears.

Aryan

"All grown up, young man," Dad said from behind as he came into my room.

"Yes dad," I replied as I turned to face him with my undone tie for my graduation ceremony.

"Aryan, today's a big day. I always had expectations from you and you have never failed me. After this graduation, I now want you, to start looking after our business too. I also wanted to ask you, if you really want to take over the business or do you want something else?" he asked, helping me with my tie.

"Our business is my dream too, Dad. Just like you have taken it to greater heights, I have always wanted to do the same. I'm going to take over our business and make it flourish like never before," I replied.

"I'm proud of you, Aryan. There's no better son than you. Also, treasure Chahat. She's one great girl," he replied.

"I will. I promise. I love her and will be with her, no matter what," I replied.

Dad patted my back, and just then, Chahat came.

"Aryan… oops, sorry, I'll come later," Chahat said when she saw Dad.

"No, no, Chahat, come," Dad said.

"Thank you, Uncle," she said, smiling and coming inside.

"You both talk, I'm going downstairs. Be there in 15 minutes," he said and went outside.

We replied with an okay before he left, closing the door after him.

"I love you," I said, kissing Chahat's cheek and pulling her closer to me.

"I love you too. I'm proud of you," she said. I hugged her tightly.

"I'm going to treasure you and always make you proud," I told her, or more like promised her.

"I believe you." Her words for some reason made me happy like they were what I have always wanted to hear.

Someone who believes in me, someone who loves me. I never thought angels existed, but Chahat makes me realise that angels do exist. She's a real and authentic spirit on whom this big, bad world still hasn't managed to have any of its effect.

"Aryan, what are you thinking?" Chahat said, snapping her fingers.

"Nothing Chahat. Let's go," I said and we together went down and met my parents.

From there we directly went to the graduation ceremony where Siddhant, Abhi and Kaira were already present along with their parents. We all met each other and together went to the ceremony. Once the ceremony was over, we were showered with love and good wishes.

"I'm so proud of you," Mom said as she hugged me.

"Me too, son!" Dad said and patted my back.

"Congratulations!"Chahat said after them.

I slowly walked to her, hugged her and whispered, "Thank you, I love you" in her ear.

As I pulled away, I met Siddhant and Abhi.

"We did this!" We three said and did a high-five together.

After that, we all went for lunch where all of our parents showered us with gifts. Chahat's mom had sent a bracelet, almost the same as the one she had gifted to Chahat, and I realised that they were a set and completed each other. Chahat gifted me a tuxedo that looked just perfect! After lunch, our parents went home, leaving us with each other. After about two hours of talking and laughing, Chahat's phone rang.

"Hello? Yes, dad... I'm on my way home," Chahat said on her phone.

"Guys, I'll have to go home. My aunt is coming today, but I had a great time! Thanks a lot, and again, congratulations to all of you," Chahat said.

"Thank you!" everyone said.

Chahat left along with Kaira.

"I'm happy for you both," Siddhant said, suddenly making us look at him.

"You've found the perfect girls for you," he said, again.

"You'll find your perfect girl too," I said.

"I don't know man! It's been three years since I left the dating game thinking I would wait for my perfect girl, but I still haven't found her," Siddhant said.

"Why are you looking for her?" I asked.

"Huh?" he asked.

"Let your destiny get her to you. She will come only when you are destined to meet her. Looking for her won't do anything. Just wait and let time do its thing," I said.

"Maybe, that's right. Thanks bro," Siddhant said.

"Let's go and sit somewhere else," Abhi said and we got up and went to our most favourite spot since childhood in our new car.

"Time flies, doesn't it?" I asked.

"It does. Doesn't it feel like we were kids just some time back and suddenly we are graduates, all set for our further studies, and taking over our companies," Abhi said.

"True that! Guys, I have to tell you something," Siddhant said, all serious.

We looked at him, raising our eyebrows.

"I have to leave," he said suddenly. It felt like someone had just dropped a bomb.

"What?" Abhi and I said together.

"Dad and Anshul, my elder brother, want me to go to UAE and settle there with them. They said that I could do my post-graduation from UAE and start getting involved in the company," he said.

"Why didn't you tell us this earlier?" I asked.

"I got to know just a few days back and wanted to tell this to both of you today," he said. We could tell he didn't want to leave, but he had responsibilities too.

"That's totally fine! Even I won't be getting much time from now on," Abhi said.

"And me too," I said.

"Actual life starts now!" Siddhant said.

"But life won't be able to pull us apart," Abhi said.

"Definitely!" Siddhant and I said together.

We laughed and for a moment, it seemed old times were back.

Chahat

July 2011

Dear diary,

It's been a long journey, I now realise.

From a child to an adult, from a kindergarten kid to a grown-up who has finished post-graduation, it took a lot for me to never give up.

I am blessed with the best parents who are always right beside me to love me and take care of me.

Blessed with my only best friend who not only supports my every decision but has also been constant in doing so.

Blessed with the best boyfriend who is nothing like others and for whom my heart is not an object to play with. We have been together for almost five years now, and it still feels the same as day one.

What more can I possibly ask for?

I closed the diary and heaved a deep sigh. For the past two years, Aryan and I have been busier than earlier. I had been busy with my classes, and Aryan with his MBA, along with looking after his family business. These past years have flown really fast and soon after clearing my NET, I will start looking for a job in some university as a lecturer.

I shook my head and lay down on the bed, not realising when I went off to sleep.

The next day, Aryan had a day off and we decided to spend the day together along with Kaira and Abhi.

"Mom, Dad, I am going to the mall with Kaira, Aryan and Abhi," I said, as I went downstairs.

"Okay, enjoy yourself," they said and I nodded and went out to find Aryan, looking handsome as ever, near his car, waiting for me.

"Hi handsome!" I said, as I reached him.

"Hi beautiful!" he said, as he hugged me and lifted me a bit, making me laugh.

"I love your laugh," he said, kissing the corner of my lips.

"And I love you," I said, pecking his lips.

Just then his phone rang and he picked that up. It was probably related to business, as his expressions changed every second..

"Chahat!" he said, making me look at him.

"I've got the deal done. We've got the deal done!" he said, excited.

"Congratulations!" I said, all happy and proud.

"Thank you! It's your love that makes me want to do something for you and our future together," he said and my heart swelled at his words.

"Why do you love me so much?" I asked suddenly, because I still couldn't understand, despite spending five years with him, that how he could love me so much.

"I love you because you are absolutely one of a kind. I love you because you are 'you' and also I exist to fill you with love, affection and happiness that you are made for," he said, honesty laced in his voice.

I blushed and hid my face in his chest. He laughed, wrapped his arms around me and kissed my head.

After that, we went to the mall and met Kaira and Abhi, and we had a blast playing games at the gaming zone and eating like pigs. I had an amazing day!

∾

Soon, I started preparing for my NET exam, that would qualify me to teach in colleges, and Aryan dedicated all his time to the business. I must add that he was amazing at his work.

"Chahat, how are the preparations going?" Mom asked, coming in.

"They're going great. The exam is in two weeks," I informed.

"I know you're going to clear it with an amazing score," Mom said.

"That's true, aunty," Aryan's voice came from outside. He came inside, looking oh so handsome in his black Armani suit.

"Oh! Hi, Aryan." Mom said.

"Hi aunty!" he said.

"How come you're here today?" she asked.

"I was missing Chahat, so here I am. To see her," he said, smiling at me.

"I see what love does! You two have fun. I'll be downstairs," Mom said, smiling and closing the door after her.

"So, Mr Kapoor was missing me, huh?" I said, smirking.

"Oh yes, soon to be Mrs Kapoor," he said.

His words sent a chill down my spine. His words had an undying promise in them.

"You look cute when you blush," he said and it was then that I noticed he had removed his blazer and had kept his head on my lap.

I ran my fingers through his soft hair, played with them and lightly massaged his head. I admired his face throughout. From his soft hair down to his eyes that were closed, his eyelashes looking so long and to his perfect nose. Down there were his soft, plump lips that always looked perfect.

I looked down to see him, asleep in my lap. I took out my phone and took his photo before shifting him a bit and then covering him with my duvet.

I kissed his forehead, cheek and lips and whispered 'I love you' before putting my arms around him and closing my eyes.

Aryan

I was woken up by my phone ringing at the side. I tried to turn over, but felt something on my chest. Chahat was sleeping on my chest with her arm around me. She looked so peaceful, sleeping like a baby.

'This is going to be the best start of any day, I swear!'

I looked around to find myself on her bed and then I turned to see it was 2 p.m. I remembered coming here to be with Chahat.

I moved her a bit and turned over to see a missed call from Dad. We talked for a while before we hung up.

"Mmm," Chahat made a voice, beside me.

"Hey baby," I said, moving towards her.

"Hey," she said, smiling. "Do you have to go back?" she added softly and I could easily make out that she didn't want me to go and it made me happy.

"Yes," I lied, wanting to see her reaction.

"Oh! Okay. Great," She said, covering up her sad reaction.

"I'm kidding. I'm right here with you for the rest of the day," I said and her lips broke into a wide grin.

She hugged me tightly and kissed my cheek. The fact that we were on her bed didn't help, and we started kissing each other. I could feel her smile against my lips as we kissed. I moved on top of her and put my hands on her waist. She put her fingers in my hair and pulled them slightly, making me go crazy for her.

I slowly pulled away and kept my head near her neck slowly breathing in her scent and putting my hands under her t-shirt, touching her soft waist with my full hands. I could feel her moan as I kissed her neck and bit it lightly.

I moved down slowly and pushed her t-shirt away, exposing her shoulder to me. I kissed her shoulder and I knew I was driving her crazy.

"Chahat! Aryan!" Auntie's voice came from outside. We immediately parted and Chahat made herself look presentable as she walked to the door and opened it.

"Oh great! You both are awake. Come down for lunch," she said and went back to her work.

Chahat closed the door and came back on the bed.

"So?" I asked, awkwardly.

"So?" she replied, equally awkward.

We looked at each other and the moment our eyes met, we started laughing.

"Awkwardness doesn't suit us," I commented.

"At all," she completed, laughing.

Chahat

I opened my eyes when sunlight fell on them and slowly tried to move around, but I couldn't, since Aryan was sleeping on top of me with his head on my chest and his arms around me.

It had been almost a month since I had my NET exam and the results were to be out that day. Also, having dinners with Aryan became a frequent thing and once in a while, we would even have a sleepover together.

I smiled at him, knowing how much he loved it. He slowly opened his eyes and looked at me.

"How I want to wake up like this everyday," he said and closed his eyes again, hugging me tighter. "I hope you are comfortable," he added.

"I am, but what if I wasn't?" I asked, teasing him.

"Then I would have made you comfortable," he said.

"How?" I asked.

Without saying anything, he moved us so that he was under me and I was on top of him, making me wonder of how strong he was!

"See? Are you comfortable now?" he asked, teasing me with his sexy smirk.

"I am," I said, closing my eyes.

"And now?" he asked, putting his hands under my t-shirt and putting his hands on my waist.

I opened my eyes and I knew my cheeks were turning red and I was getting goosebumps all over my stomach. Noticing my reaction to his touch, his smirk widened.

He slowly moved his lips towards mine and I knew what he wanted. I slowly leaned in and that's when I remembered something. I moved back and hid my face in his chest.

"What happened?" he asked.

"I haven't brushed yet," I said.

"So?" he asked.

"Morning breath," I muttered.

"I don't care even a bit," he said, as he pulled me up again and kissed me hard.

I smiled against his lips, knowing he didn't care about my morning breath and that such things don't affect his love for me made me happy. It was just a small thing, but it touched me to my core and warmed my heart.

"I love you," he said against my lips.

"I love you too," I said, slowly pulling away and looking into his eyes.

For a moment, it felt like time had frozen. It was just me and him in the moment and nothing else.

"Chahat! Aryan!" Aryan's mom called out from outside.

"Yes mom?" Aryan asked.

"Get ready and come down for breakfast," she said and after we replied with an okay, we could hear her footsteps fading away.

"Let's get ready," I said, sitting up.

I had started to keep a few clothes at his place. After we got ready, we went downstairs and had breakfast with uncle and aunty before Aryan dropped me home and left for his office. I went inside, read a novel for a few hours and when the result was out, around lunch time, I checked it.

"Mom, I have cleared my NET exam. See!" I said, smiling, and showing her the result on my laptop.

"Oh my god! Amazing! Just look at the score! I'm so proud of you. I'll just give a call to your father," she said, kissing my forehead and taking her phone with her to call dad.

I immediately messaged Aryan about the result, and just on cue, his call came.

"Congratulations, Chahat! I'm so proud of you," he said, the moment I picked up the call.

"Thank you so much, Aryan," I replied, smiling.

"What's up? Why do you sound so low?" he asked.

"Nothing! I am happy." I said, or more like I convinced myself.

"Chahat, what's wrong?" He asked.

"Nothing, Aryan. Mom is here. I'll just call you back?" I asked.

"Sure, but prepare yourself to tell me what's wrong," he said before we hung up.

"Your dad is so happy. Tonight, I'm going to cook some of your favourite dishes," she said happily and went to the kitchen.

I nodded and smiled. I closed my laptop and kept it on the coffee table before closing my eyes. When I gave it a thought, it was not what I wanted. I wanted to paint. I wanted to draw. I had promised myself that I would take a job only when I felt I didn't want to live anymore, because such jobs weren't made for me. I might be alive physically, but I would be dead, mentally and emotionally.

"Chahat? The doorbell is ringing. Where are you lost?" Mom asked, opening the door.

Aryan entered and sat beside me.

"Your favourite chocolate cake to celebrate this amazing result," he said, putting a cake box on the centre table.

"Thank you!" I said, smiling.

"You're so sweet," Mom said.

"But auntie, I sense someone isn't smiling from her heart," he said.

"No. I'm good and so.... happy," I said.

"Chahat, let it out," Aryan said.

"I don't want to teach," I said.

"Why?" Mom asked.

"I cannot do this. Now that I imagine my life, going to the school, teaching and coming back is just not for me. I like teaching and to get children educated, but I can't live like that," I said.

"You should have thought about that before. Why prepare when you don't want it? You have to be serious. You have to do something in your life, Chahat. You can't say you can't live like that. Everyone has to work," Mom said, clearly disappointed.

"I don't know what was wrong with me. I never thought about this before today. I am sorry," I said, feeling guilty.

Just then, Aryan's hand found way to my hand and held it.

"Auntie, don't ask her such questions. It happens and she once mentioned about it to me too," he said, covering up.

"Don't lie, Aryan. You always take her side," Mom said.

"Auntie, I am not. Some years back when I asked Chahat about what her life should be like, she said that she can't imagine herself in some 9 to 5 job. Maybe, it didn't just have to be from 9 to 5, but any job that involves repeating the same routine. It is not her thing and she just realised it now," Aryan said, immediately coming to my rescue. I couldn't thank him more for that.

Mom thought for a while.

"Auntie, I promised myself that I'll fulfil each and every dream of hers and make her the happiest girl alive. If teaching is not a part of her dream, then let it be. She can and will do whatever she wants because it will make her happy. I work hard only because I want to do something for her. So that she's proud of me. I left a meeting to come here only because I knew she was sounding low, which is rare," he said.

I was about to cry and would have kissed him hard if mom wasn't there. I looked at him wondering how I got so lucky. How can he love me so much? And I knew mom was thinking the same.

"You love her like she's your own baby or maybe even more than that," Mom joked.

"She's my little one, auntie," he said, patting my head.

'And everyone, jolly Aryan is back,' I thought.

Mom laughed and asked whether I really thought that about 9 to 5 jobs.

"Yes mom. I'll take such jobs when I will quit the idea of feeling alive," I said.

"Stop saying that, will you? After what happened years back, don't say this please," Mom said, remembering the past. I immediately apologised and Aryan changed the topic.

"But what do you want to do? You know you will have to do something in your life, right?" Mom asked.

"I want to paint and create some masterpieces and earn from that," I said, happily.

"As if it's that easy," Mom said, clearly concerned.

"It's not, but at least I'll be happy and it's not like I won't work hard. I'll work hard and make you all proud. Maybe I won't earn a lot, but I'll be happy," I said.

"Let's not get this earning thing here, Chahat. You know you don't have to think about such a thing when I am here," Aryan said.

"I know, but still, it is a matter to think about," I said, squeezing his hand.

"Earning is not a problem. Your father earns a lot and also, you are great at painting. I know some people do earn a lot from this." Mom finally said something positive about my decision.

"So, can I go for it?" I asked, hopefully.

"Yes, you can, as long as you are happy and if it doesn't work out for you, then you always can opt for teaching in future," Mom said.

"Oh yes! I can," I said, smiling.

"So, can you cut the cake now?" Aryan asked.

"Oh yes! Get me something to cut this cake, you fat ass," I said to Aryan.

"Whatever, kid," he said.

"Shut up and move a bit, tall man," I said.

"You both sit, the maid is here and she'll do the rest," Mom said.

After cutting the cake and spending half an hour with us, Aryan left for work.

~

I finished with my painting and sighed happily after looking at my work. That was so appealing to my eyes!

I was so happy with my life for the past few months, because I could paint whenever I wanted to and also, I earned from it enough that I didn't have to depend on my parents.

My phone started to ring, bringing me back from my thoughts.

"Hello, Ms Aggarwal. How are you?" Mr Singh asked me.

"I'm good, Mr Singh. How are you?" I asked.

"I'm good. I wanted to inform you that all the paintings you gave us are sold, and as always, you'll be getting 50 percent of it," he said.

"Oh my god! Thank you so much. I'll be sending someone tomorrow to deliver all the new paintings to your gallery. He'll collect the money on my behalf," I said.

"Sure, Ms Aggarwal. Have a good day," he said and after bidding goodbye, we hung up.

I called Aman, the delivery person who always packed and delivered the paintings for me. Over the months that had passed, he had become more of a friend to me. He was loyal, hardworking and trustworthy.

"Hey Chahat. A delivery again?" he asked when I called him.

"Hey Aman. Yes, come over tomorrow, I'll help you pack them and then you have to deliver them. Also, please collect a packet from Mr Singh and give it to me," I said.

"Sure. I'll be there by 12," he said.

"Okay. Thank you," I said.

After ending the call, I sat down and thought about how beautifully things had fallen into place from the time I had decided that this was exactly what I was going to do. I did what I loved and I was not just satisfied, but also extremely happy about it.

My phone rang and I picked it up, after seeing it was Aryan.

"I miss you," he breathed on the other side, making my heart skip a beat.

"Long time no see! I miss you too," I said, playing with him.

"Oh yes! When did we meet last?" he asked, playing along.

"Like a day back?" I asked.

"Oh my god! So long," he said, seriously.

"Is it a sarcastic comment?" I asked.

"No really! Every second without you feels like a year," he said.

"What a flirt!" I commented, nonchalantly.

"Only with you. Anyway, Abhi wants to see us both," he said.

"Oh great. When?" I asked.

"Tonight. I'll pick you up at 8. It will be fine, right?" he asked.

"Absolutely. I can't wait to see you and him too," I said.

After talking for a bit, we hung up and I passed my time thinking about my next paintings. Around 7, I started to get ready and wore my red cut-sleeve top tucked in my black bell bottoms with a pair of block comfortable heels. I kept my hair open and took my sling.

Around 8, Aryan was there and we went to see Abhi. After reaching the restaurant, we looked around to spot him in a corner. We went to him and Aryan hugged him. I shook his hand before we sat down.

"Okay, so guys, let's get this straight, I am planning to propose to Kaira," he said.

"What?" Aryan and I said together, not expecting that.

"Oh my god! Are you serious?" I asked, excited, happy for Kaira, and why not! She deserved every bit of happiness and I knew Abhi was going to give her that! Kaira, Diya, Samaira and I have been inseparable since our school days and I just couldn't be happier for her than I was then.

"Yes! I am very serious," he said and I could tell he actually was serious. His eyes reflected the love he felt for her.

"Are you serious?" Aryan asked.

"Yes. I know Siddhant and you would react like this, but man, I really am serious," he said.

"That's great, but Abhi, you are just 25," Aryan said.

"I know, but tell me something, if you are told to marry Chahat right now, will you marry her?" Abhi asked and my heart started beating faster. I got all nervous and I looked at Aryan anxiously.

"Obviously I will. She's the one who has made me what I am. She's mine for eternity and I won't think twice before marrying her," he said and I looked down. My cheeks turned red, my heart was pounding and I felt goosebumps on my skin.

It was different to hear it from him. It was better when he said it. I smiled and I felt my heart was smiling along too.

"That's it, man. I feel the same. There's nothing forcing me; it's something that comes from the inside, telling me it's time. I just want to put my ring on her finger to mark her mine. If she wants to get married after a year or two, I am okay, but as for me, I think it's time to get her surname changed," Abhi said. I smiled as I imagined Kaira as a bride.

Suddenly a name popped in my mind.

It wasn't Chahat Aggarwal. It was Chahat Aryan Kapoor. My heart smiled again.

After that, we gave our suggestions and after dinner we all left. Abhi would be proposing to her after a week, and I just couldn't wait!

"I'm just so happy," I said, as Aryan and I were on our way back.

"Me too. It's so satisfying to see him happy and finally settling down," he said.

"I can't wait for this moment to come in our lives, Chahat," he added and I blushed.

"Me too," I whispered.

"Will you marry me?" he said suddenly.

"You just did not!" I said, all straight and in a loud voice.

"Woman! Has this surprised you?" he asked.

"No! Mr Aryan Kapoor, don't you dare propose me like this! You better plan a surprise for me," I said.

"God! Chahat! I will plan a surprise! Don't worry," he said, laughing.

"And get a photographer too! I want him to capture every single moment," I said, folding my arms and mentally imagining how it all would be like.

"As you say, baby," he said, smiling and laughing.

We reached home and I kissed him before I got out of the car.

The next week passed in a blur and then came the day when Abhi was going to propose to Kaira.

We helped Abhi in implementing the plan and we all together watched how Kaira was shocked and went wide-eyed to Abhi on his one knee with a ring in hand.

When he expressed how his life changed from the moment she came in his life and told her how much he loved her, Kaira cried out of happiness. Well, Diya and I wept too.

When Kaira said yes, Abhi put a ring on her finger and all the party poppers went off, making the moment special. It looked beautiful and very magical. We congratulated the couple and after we spent some time with them both, we decided to leave them alone.

I couldn't help but notice the glow on Kaira's face and the shine in her eyes. It made her look even more beautiful than she already was. I was so happy for her that I couldn't express it in mere words.

∾

"I'm so glad to hear that people are loving my paintings," I said to Mr Singh.

"You won't believe it, every person who lays his eyes on your paintings, becomes a fan!" he said excitedly.

"It's so good to know that. So, I'll get back to you when the paintings are ready," I said.

"Take your time, dear. Bless you. Bye," he said.

"Thank you. Bye," I said.

Just as I hung up, Kaira called me.

"And, and, and, get your dresses ready because 16 November is a big day," she said, just the moment I picked up the phone.

"Oh my god! Congratulations! I am so happy for you!" I said, excited.

"Thank you so much!" she said.

"But it's so close. Will you be able to make all the preparations for the wedding?" I asked.

"Oh, yes. It's a destination wedding in Jodhpur. So, those people are experts at it, babe!" she said.

"So, my best friend is going to be all dolled up like a princess and get married to her prince in a palace?" I asked.

"Something like that!" she said and I knew she would be blushing.

"I love the idea of it," I said, honestly.

"I know, right! Okay, so I want my school gang with me on all the functions of my wedding. I don't care," she said.

"Okay woman! Diya and I will surely be there and I'll ask Samaira," I said.

"No asking! She has to be there. We were inseparable in school and it's going to be nothing different at my wedding. Give me Samaira's number, I'll give her a call," she said.

I gave her the number and I already knew Samaira was going to be there, because winning an argument with Kaira was impossible.

The next day, I got a call from Samaira. She told me she was coming to India the next month and then we would be attending Kaira's wedding. The good thing was that she was going to be in Mumbai permanently, but that would be until she got hitched. I really, really hoped that she had a love story like that of a romance fiction novel with a happily ever after. After all, she deserved every bit of it. I started working on my paintings faster than before because I was going to take a break in November.

I was working when my phone rang, showing Aryan's call.

"Hey babe," I said, keeping my palette aside.

"Hey babe. Abhi called and guess what," he said.

"What?" I asked excitedly.

"Not telling you," he said.

"What? You can't do that," I said.

"You want to know?" he asked.

"Of course," I said.

"Then pop in the car that is parked outside your house. Bye. Love you," he said and hung up.

I shook my head and after wearing my flip flops went outside and spotted Aryan's car. I went in the passenger seat and turned to him.

"Now?" I asked, smiling.

"Let me see you properly at least," he said, not even blinking his eyes.

"Oh god, Aryan!" I said, blushing, making him laugh.

"This is for my lady," he said and he put his hand on the back seat of car and took out a bouquet and my favourite fries.

"I love you!" I said, kissing him and pulling away and grabbing my gifts.

"I was craving some," I said, as I started eating the fries after smelling the amazing bouquet of flowers.

"Well, I know my girl too well, don't I?" he said, smiling and kissing my forehead.

"Oh yes! You do," I said.

"And yes, Abhi and Kaira have planned a proper holiday in Goa for all of us," He said.

"They what?" I asked, excited.

"They have planned a holiday for us all in Goa," he said, smiling after seeing me so excited.

I shouted a 'woohoo'.

"But why would they have their honeymoon with us?" I asked the dumbest question ever.

He shook his head and told me that they'll leave for their honeymoon after this holiday in Goa. I nodded and we decided to have a night ride before he dropped me home.

∾

"Mr Singh, I've sent all the paintings to your gallery. Just drop me a message when you get them," I said on the call.

"Of course. You have a blast at your friend's wedding," Mr Singh said on the other side.

"Thank you so much. I'll start working on new paintings after I come back a month later," I said.

"Yes, don't worry. Have fun, dear," he said and we hung up.

I decided to surprise Aryan at his office.

I changed my dress and took my bag and left for his office. I reached there after half an hour and went to his office straightaway.

His assistant told me he was inside. I knocked and went in. As I entered, I saw his back was towards me and he was on his phone. I waited till he was done before I tiptoed behind him and hugged him tightly.

He was rigid at first, but after he knew it was me, he relaxed and turned around.

"Surprise," I whispered and kissed his cheek, his beard tickling my cheeks.

"You know how much I love your surprises," he said and hugged me tightly.

"I know, Aryan," I said and he kissed my cheek. "So? Are you done?" I asked as I moved towards his desk.

He sat down on his seat and pulled me on his lap.

"Almost through. Don't worry, I'll finish before we leave," he said.

"Good. I'm so excited," I said, smiling.

"Me too. We would have some quality time to spend together, Chahat. Also, I can't wait for Abhi to turn from a bachelor to a married guy. First one amongst the three of us to get married," he said, smiling happily. Their friendship was amazing.

"By the way, when is Samaira coming?" he continued, playing with my hair.

"This Saturday," I replied, happily.

He smiled at me. After that I got up and went to the couch while he completed his work. After he was done, we went to a restaurant and had our dinner there before he dropped me home. His driver had dropped my car at my place already. The next few days of the week passed in a blink of an eye and before I knew it, Samaira landed in India. We planned to meet at central mall at 3 p.m.

I changed into a pair of jeans and an off-shoulder top and went to the mall. Just as I entered, I spotted Samaira and ran towards her. I took her into a bone-crushing hug and she hugged me back as tightly as she could. After that, we shopped and I helped Samaira with all the things that were left to pack for Kaira's wedding. After we spent the whole day at the mall, we went back to our homes.

"Hey pig," I said as Aryan picked my call.

"Hey kid," he said and he sounded tired.

"What's up?" I asked.

"Nothing, just a bit tired because I had to finish all the stuff today as we won't be here during the majority of the next month," he said.

"Right. At least you're now free and won't be taking your work along," I said.

"I won't. By the way, how's Samaira?" he asked.

"She's amazing," I said and I went on telling him about the day, and all the gossip I got from Samaira about the people we knew. He sat there, listening to my blabbering and telling me that he didn't know half of the people I was telling him about. We talked for a bit more before saying goodnight.

The next day, Kaira and Abhi had decided to host a party at

Abhi's place before we left for their destination wedding. Samaira and I went together and we all had a blast. Samaira met everyone after so many years. Aryan, Abhi, Kaira, Diya and I planned to make Samaira and Siddhant meet. My dearest, dearest best friend had always had a crush on Siddhant.

We all left them alone to get to know each other, and unlike what we expected, they both seemed to have hit it off in an instant. I already knew right then, if not a couple, they both were going to be really good friends.

The good thing about all of it was that they both won't be feeling awkward around each other, because in Jodhpur, we all were going to hang out together. After we were done, Samaira left with Siddhant while I went home.

The next day, the flight to Jodhpur got cancelled due to some issues and Aryan, Sid, Sam and I decided to go to Jodhpur by train. We couldn't afford to skip even a single function, or Abhi and Kaira would kill us.

We had an amazing time while we were traveling to Jodhpur. I even dozed off while travelling, with my head on Aryan's shoulder.

When we reached Jodhpur, Samaira and I went to our room while Aryan and Sid went to theirs.

After we got comfortable in our bed, Samaira and I had a talk where she told me about Siddhant.

"I don't know why it felt so good to talk to him," she said, smiling.

"Oh, my! Is this the tenth standard Samaira talking to me?" I asked.

"No. It's the mature one talking," she replied, smiling. "How do you feel around Aryan?" she asked, again.

"Aryan? Honestly, hearing his name itself gives me butterflies. Whenever I am around him, I don't have to pretend at all. I can be myself because for all I know, he won't judge me. He kisses my hand, he smiles at me whenever I catch him looking at me, he makes me feel like I am the only girl for him and he makes me feel tremendously special. He also never forgets to tell me how much he loves me and how much he wants to marry me. After all, there's a reason why even after eight years, we are still strong and in love like day one. I sometimes even wonder – how can he love me this much?" I said, smiling.

"Wow, you guys are actually couple goals stuff. Chahat, what can you do for him?" she asked, all awake.

"Me? Anything. One thing I have always promised myself is that I will be pure for Aryan, because a pure guy like him, deserves only a pure girl. For him and his happiness, I can even break my own heart and leave him," I said, determined.

"Pure?" she asked.

"By pure, I mean a girl who has nothing to do with cruelty. Someone who hasn't hurt anyone in her life, who only wants good for everyone. I know Aryan is like that and I want him to get a girl exactly like that," I said.

"You know, you are pure," Samaira said.

"I don't know," I said, laughing.

"Yes, you are," Samaira said, smiling.

"I know you'll find someone like this; about whom you just won't be able to stop talking. Someone you'll be ready to do anything and everything for, without a second thought. For whom you'll always only want the best. Sam, when you get him, don't do anything that makes you go away from him. Love him, cherish him and give him nothing less than the best of yourself," I said.

"Thank you, Chahat and I promise I will keep that in my mind," she said. "But you actually are head over heels in love with Aryan," Samaira continued.

"I truly am," I accepted, blushing.

Soon after, we went to sleep. The next day we forced Abhi to give us something to do. To be together, Aryan and I chose one task, leaving Samaira and Siddhant to take another one. After completing the tasks we were given, we went back to the hotel and got ready for the club, where they were throwing a little bachelor's party. We reached the club and Aryan and I danced like there was no tomorrow.

A slow song played and Aryan and I swayed in each other's arms and it was the best feeling ever. It felt like forever when we stayed in each other's arms. I knew that he was the one I wanted for life. He was the one with whom I would not mind laughing when we get old. He was the one I would not mind spending my entire life with.

"Gosh! You two are extremely cute. Honestly, couple goals," someone said from behind.

We came out of our trance and turned to that girl. We muttered a 'thank you' before Kaira waved at me, telling me it was late and we needed to leave.

I nodded and took Aryan's hand in mine and moved out. I looked behind to see Sam and Sid in each other's arms. Aryan saw the same and we smirked, having some idea of what could have happened. As much as we loved seeing them like that, we needed to go. We called and told them that it was late and we had to leave. After reaching back, we directly went to sleep because from the next day, the functions for Kaira's wedding would start.

The next day, we got ready for the function to be held. Kaira looked amazing in her dress. She had always been beautiful, but she had a different glow.

"I can't wait to see us like that," Aryan said beside me.

I looked ahead and spotted Kaira and Abhi, sitting down performing the rituals. Their parents were around them and they all were laughing at something. I was happy to see them laugh.

"Me too," I said, honestly.

I couldn't wait to be Aryan's bride and tie the knot with him in the presence of our family and friends. The function was amazing, but surprisingly, we were not really tired like we imagined to be. Aryan and I decided to go to a mall since I needed to buy some stuff. I changed but spotted Samaira who was sad and deep in thought. I asked her many times and after she forced me to go, I didn't have any option. She needed time and I understood that, but it didn't mean she could get away with that. She had to tell me. After we shopped and had our dinner, I had an immediate need to use the loo.

"Aryan, I have to use the loo. I'll be back in a bit," I said.

He nodded and stood outside the washroom while I went inside.

I washed my hands after I was done and opened the door, only to see a pretty girl in front of Aryan. And just as suddenly, she kissed him with all her might. Aryan had his hands on her waist. The moment I saw this, my jaw fell to the floor. My vision became blurry. I could feel my tears building up.

'What did just happen?'

'How could he do this?'

"Chahat!" I heard Aryan calling me worriedly, and I looked up in disgust to see that girl smirking, still beside Aryan.

I didn't reply because tears and disappointment in my eyes were enough to make him know that the damage was done. I moved past them.

"Chahat! Listen to me. Please... don't cry. It's not what it looks like," he said as he came after me.

"What? All I saw was that girl kissing you. How do you want me to interpret it?" I asked, turning around.

"Chahat, I know it seems wrong but—" he started.

"But what? You had your hands on her waist. Maybe she forcefully kissed you, but didn't you find the need to push her away?" I asked, angry and hurt.

Maybe I was overreacting or just trying not to hear. I couldn't help but remember that moment again and again. I never thought I would witness such an incident in my entire life.

When he didn't reply, I turned around. I started to move away from him and reached the exit of the mall when he started calling after me yet again. I spotted a taxi nearby and I was about to enter it when Aryan held my wrist. Not finding any other way out, I turned around to face him. My heart broke when I saw sheer pain in his eyes. His eyes were red and I knew he was about to cry at any moment now.

"I need time. Leave me alone," I said, as I looked at the ground.

"You don't trust me?" he said, suddenly, and he was sounding broken.

I didn't reply to that and suddenly his hold on my wrist loosened and I knew he was letting me go. That action was a little thing, but it held a great impact. I turned around without looking at him again and sat in the taxi and gave the taxi driver the name of the resort.

There was no stopping my tears the moment I sat in the taxi. I broke down and I cried hard.

Has he gotten bored of me?

Wasn't I enough for him?

Didn't he mean it when he said he wanted me forever?

I felt my heart was shattered into a million small pieces. My world seemed like it had stopped.

Maybe he was enjoying himself like that.

Maybe he was enjoying kissing her.

I kept crying, and in no time, I reached the resort.

I entered our room and saw Samaira. She immediately came to my rescue and handled me before she gave me water.

She kept asking what had happened. After I told her what happened, she went outside in search of Aryan and even hit Aryan on his face. It was exceedingly surprising and at that moment, I couldn't help but feel protective about him. No matter what he did, I still loved him!

That night, Samaira gave me my own space to introspect and between it all, I didn't know exactly when I fell asleep.

The next day, I told Kaira and Diya about what had happened before we went for the function. They were very angry and wanted to talk to him, but I stopped them because I had left it all on destiny. Well, that's what I got from introspecting. During the function, I tried paying attention to the rituals and at the same time, was trying not to look at Aryan. I could tell, the bruised eye was fine, but he was very silent, showing how he was affected by the incident.

A part of me was saying that Aryan didn't kiss her back, and I judged him without knowing what really had happened; but the other part of me wasn't ready to accept it as that image was coming back to my head.

The entire day went on like that before Siddhant called us all in his room and said he wanted to propose to Samaira. It wasn't expected at all and despite all the sadness, there was finally a reason to be happy.

The next day, I helped Kaira with all the basic preps and when she told me to get my red dress from my room, I agreed to that. Suddenly the door closed and it was locked. I turned around to look at the door when I heard a voice, behind me.

Aryan's voice, to be precise.

Aryan

The moment she sat in the taxi and went away, I was broken. I wanted to cry. I wanted to run after her and tell her the reality, but I didn't. I thought, out of all the people in this world, my Chahat would believe me. She would trust me, but I was wrong. Instead of listening to me, she went away.

I took another taxi and went to the resort. The moment I entered the room, I went to the washroom to let my tears fall. I cried, I cried really hard.

I can't live without her, but how could she not trust me?

How could she not hear my explanation?

I cried for a while, then came out and suddenly was greeted with a punch by Samaira. I heard Chahat and Sid shout my name.

I looked at Chahat and saw nothing but worry in her eyes for me. She cared, she still cared for me.

Siddhant asked for an explanation when we were alone and I told him honestly that it was Swapna, the girl who had a huge crush on me from college. She got emotional and forced herself on me when I told her I am with Chahat, my girlfriend.

After knowing I was not at fault in the entire situation, Siddhant consoled me that Chahat was just as sad as me and hurt and deserved her time. I agreed and smiled sadly at the reality before I slept.

The next day passed in a blink. I didn't realise when I was talking, when I was eating, when I was walking and when I was sleeping.

That night, Siddhant told us all that he wanted to propose Samaira. I was really happy for him. Finally, my best friend had found his match. Chahat was also there and only I knew how it hurt me when she wasn't even ready to look at me.

The next day, I was helping out Siddhant with his proposal when he told me to get Samaira's planner from her room. I was resistant about the whole thing but had to get it for him anyway. Just as I entered and was looking for it, the door behind me closed.

I turned to see Chahat there, looking at the door in confusion.

"Chahat," I said.

She looked at me in shock.

"You planned this!" we both said to each other at the same time.

We stayed quiet and knew right then that it was our friends' idea.

"I'm sorry," I started, feeling I had to start despite how much I wanted her to have her time.

"You don't have to," Chahat said.

"No, I have to. I am sorry I didn't try to explain this to you earlier," I started, being honest. "I didn't explain it all before because I thought you needed your own time and space, to gather yourself and to realise it yourself how much I love you, and that I would never do such a thing,"

"I trusted you. If I wouldn't have trusted you, why would I even say that I need time? I would have simply broken up with you and left. If I wouldn't have trusted you, then by now, I would have managed to be out of this room and not be standing here and talking to you," Chahat said and a tear dropped from her eye.

It broke me the moment I saw a tear in her eye. I moved towards her and took her face in my hands as I slowly wiped the tears from her face. It was then that I realised how much I loved her. It was then that I knew that I could handle anything that this world threw at me, but I couldn't tolerate a tear in Chahat's eyes. It was just a day, but it felt like eternity. I missed her voice. I missed her smile. I missed her laugh. I missed everything about her.

I was lifeless the whole day without her, and then I knew that she was the oxygen that kept me alive. She made me feel alive. I was a zombie with no life, with no aim, with no reason without her.

"Swapna is her name. She forced herself on me. She had a huge crush on me since we were in the same college. She met me there yesterday after years and when I told her I was there waiting for you, she became emotional and maybe when she heard the door of the washroom opening, she purposely kissed me out of the blue. I was in shock because I wasn't expecting that, but then I pushed her away and saw you there, crying with your head hung down," I said as I held her face in my hands.

"I love you, Chahat. I always have and I always will. I never cheated on you. It was timing. It was that stupid girl who created this misunderstanding. I am sorry I thought you didn't trust me and it broke me because the foundation of a relationship is trust. I became lifeless after you left. I felt my world had stopped when you left," I said and by the time it ended, I couldn't control myself and started crying.

Chahat looked at me and hugged me tightly.

"Aryan, I am here. I won't go anywhere. I am also sorry. My feelings were so messed up. I couldn't think about anything but just the fact that she was kissing you. I never expected to be in such a situation and it caught me completely off guard. I am really sorry, Aryan. My heart was broken into a million pieces. My world had stopped too. I wasn't even looking forward to the next day. It's now that I realise I am nothing without you. My life has no meaning without you. Aryan Kapoor, I love you and I promise that I am never going away. I'll always be with you. Always," Chahat said as she cried, with me in her arms.

I held onto her tightly. She was everything I had. She was everything I would ever want.

Chahat

After Aryan and I sorted out our misunderstanding, we were inseparable. We got to know that there was no way that we could be without each other. He was the part of me without which I was not myself.

It was now that after crying with him for the first time, I felt love in a completely different and unique way.

The wedding day was finally here and we helped Kaira pack and calm down her pre-wedding jitters before we left to get ready.

"Chahat, you ready?" Samaira asked.

"No. Sam, can you please call Aryan?" I asked.

She nodded and in no time, Aryan was there.

"How do I look?" I asked as I twirled in front of him. That was the dress he had chosen for me.

"Better than I imagined," he said.

I smiled brightly at him and I turned to put on my earrings. I felt Aryan hugging me from behind.

"My pretty girl," he said as he nuzzled my neck with his nose.

I smiled at him through the mirror.

"You're going to kill me one day with that smile," he said.

"Not so fast, baby. There are many more things left to do," I said, boldly. My boldness shocked both of us.

"Woah. That sounded sensual," he remarked.

"Maybe because it was meant to," I said as I winked and started walking towards the door.

"You're definitely going to be my death," he said as he came after me.

I went to Kaira's room while Aryan left to be with Abhi.

"You look gorgeous," I said as I couldn't take my eyes off Kaira.

"Thank you so much," she said as she smiled.

We went to the wedding hall and all the rituals took place there, and soon, Kaira and Abhi became a married couple.

The next day, we went to the airport and took our flight to Goa and reached there around 7 p.m. We checked into the hotel, had our dinner and slept. The next day, I helped Samaira get ready as she had to meet Siddhant's family. After they left, we all decided to have a lazy day at the hotel's beach. We swam, splashed water. It was all the more fun after Samaira and Siddhant joined us.

"Chahat, I have shifted your luggage to my room," Aryan said as we were walking back to our room.

"What about Sam?" I asked.

"Siddhant will be with her," Aryan said and smirked.

I laughed thinking about her reaction as we entered the room.

"I'm going for a shower first," I said, taking off my see-through white top, exposing my long line bralette as it was completely wet and I couldn't stand a moment more in it.

"Don't tease me, Chahat!" Aryan groaned.

I was confused but realised that taking off my top easily turned Aryan on.

"Before you say something, it was not intentional," I said but I knew the damage was done as Aryan walked towards me. I started to move back as he came closer.

"Oh yeah?" he said, smirking as he was in front of me and my back had touched the wall.

I couldn't speak as I was lost in his eyes. Slowly, his hands moved to my waist and he held my waist with both his warm hands. I felt someone just let loose about a thousand butterflies in my stomach. My skin burned at the places he touched me. He slowly pinched my skin and I groaned, but to my surprise, it sounded more like a moan.

His eyes darkened and suddenly he started kissing me hard. His kiss had an urgency and I responded to it with all my might. I kissed him back with equal intensity. His hands wandered all over my stomach and my back while my hands found their way to his hair. I pulled his hair, which earned me a groan from him.

Somewhere in between our intimacy, we got rid of his wet shirt too and my hands were now on his warm chest. We continued it for a while... kissing, caressing, touching and also saying sweet words in the middle of it.

As we pulled away, we placed our foreheads together and were breathing fast.

"That was intense," he remarked, to which I nodded with my eyes closed.

I opened my eyes and his chest came in view and I realised that my boyfriend had an amazing body with abs that could have girls at his mercy easily.

I blushed. He held my chin and made me look up. He kissed my forehead and my cheek.

"Go and take a shower baby, before you catch a cold," he said, smiling and winking at me.

I blushed but went to the washroom anyway.

Aryan

After our moment, I couldn't help but realise that Chahat was someone I couldn't resist. Her skin was beyond soft. It felt like silk under my hands. She was gorgeous in every way, her beauty was unmatched and the innocence was another add-on.

Chahat walked out with her hair wet, in her crop top and shorts. Her cheeks were a bit pink and I was not sure whether it was from our moment earlier or because of the hot shower. I took a cold shower myself before we both went to have dinner. After we came back, I went to bed with my arm around Chahat's waist and her back to my chest.

The next morning, I got up to spot Chahat sleeping on my chest, soundly. I smiled at the sight and just adored her. She looked like an angel even in her sleep! I decided to get ready. After I got out from the shower, I was expecting to see her awake, but instead, she was still sleeping soundly. I sat beside her and started to pamper her with kisses all over her face, making her giggle in her sleep. I was about to move towards her lips, when she suddenly woke up.

"Why did you wake me up?" she asked, rubbing her eyes.

"Come on! It's late. By the way, you should appreciate that I woke you up in such a sweet manner," I said.

"Yeah right. I'm going back to sleep and don't disturb me," she said as she plopped down on the bed. Again.

"It's 9 o'clock already," I pointed out.

"You talk like it's 10 o'clock," she said.

"But still," I continued and she just ignored me by closing her eyes. "You're going to pay for this," I said as I started to tickle her. She started laughing very hard and was at my mercy in less than a minute.

"Okay, okay!" she said as it was becoming unbearable for her.

The next two days passed in a blink as we did a whole lot of sightseeing, went to casinos and the game parlour. We also attended a totally insane beach party on the last day.

We slept early that night because we had to catch a flight back to Mumbai early next morning.

Chahat

After we had a memorable time at the wedding, I got busy with my paintings, while Aryan got busy with his company. We didn't meet for three days, but after that, we met on a regular basis like before.

He changed his schedule and before going to office, he started stopping by, met me for 5-10 minutes and then left for office.

I just loved him so much for that!

My alarm buzzed and I got up. I brushed, combed my hair as I heard the honk of Aryan's car. I smiled and went down. I hugged him as I saw him in his suit, all ready for work.

"Have an amazing day, baby," I said.

"I will, because my day has been starting amazingly for the past few days," he said as he hugged me tighter.

We stayed like that for a while and then I kissed his cheek and he left for work.

I was having my breakfast when Mom told me that she and Dad and would be away for a month to attend my cousin sister's wedding in America.

"When will you leave?" I asked.

"Today. We'll leave for the airport in an hour," she said.

"What?" I asked.

"Don't tell me you forgot again, Chahat. We told you this a month back," she said.

"Right. Sorry. Have you packed?" I asked.

"Yes, we have," she said.

Soon, Dad was there and they both were ready to leave.

"Take care, my love. Be safe," Mom said as she hugged me.

"She's my champ. She'll be strong and she'll take care of herself," Dad said.

"I will. Take care you two," I said as I hugged Dad.

"We will. We love you always. You are very precious and we are proud of you," they said as they sat in the car and left for the airport.

I went back inside and continued working on my painting when I got a message from Diya.

Diya: *What's up, girl? My brother is organising a party. You have to be there.*

Chahat: *Of course! I'll be there. Details?*

Diya: *Hotel Grand. 8:00 p.m. Dress code: White.*

I replied with an okay and after painting for some more time, I started getting ready. I wore a white and gold dress with my gold heels. I left my hair open and put on some make up.

I reached the venue and called Diya.

"Hi Chahat. Have you reached?" she asked.

"Yes, I have. Where are you?" I asked.

"I am inside. The party's in the big lawn in the backside. Ask someone about the lawn. They'll guide you. Hurry!" she said.

"Okay. Bye," I said.

I went inside and to my surprise, there was a big box.

I looked at the guide and he pointed to the box.

I opened it and all of a sudden, many red heart, circle and other shapes of balloons came out and floated in the sky. I looked at them, smiling, and found that some of the balloons were stuck to the box, so they just stayed at their spot and moved with the breeze.

When the last balloon of the box came up, I found a message written on it: 'Turn Around.'

The wind started blowing faster than before and my hair went along with it.

I turned and found the biggest shock of my life. I found Aryan on one knee with a velvet ring box in his hand. As the wind was blowing, the fire crackers went off. They were so many that they lit up the place.

"3 March 2006, the last day of our school, I saw you for the first time. You were walking with books in your hand which blocked your view and as I was a 'moron with no eyes', I didn't see you. I am glad I didn't see you, because it was because of that I noticed you. I was drawn to you; I was attracted to you. It was the first time I wanted to talk to someone. I put my ego away for the first time and messaged you. We became friends and I started to look for different ways to be with you, to make you smile, to make you feel special. When I realised my feelings, I proposed to you. You neither denied nor accepted," he started and I laughed to that.

"We went on until I got a call from you to meet you in the same park. I got the biggest surprise when you proposed to me. That day marked the start of our relationship. There was no looking back after it. We graduated, finished our post-graduation and started working together. I have witnessed some big events of my life with you, Chahat and I want to continue doing that. I have never met someone like you. You are innocent, pure, kind, beautiful, talented, gorgeous, generous, funny and compassionate. People like you are rare in today's world," he said, and by that time, I was crying.

"You laugh at my lamest jokes, you scold me whenever I get a wound, but always come with a first aid, you hold me tightly when I am crying, you are the happiest when I achieve something, and you love me like no one else. You make me strong; you make me want to be the best. You are the reason behind my success, you are the reason behind my smile, my laugh, my face's glow. You are an amazing best friend, an amazing daughter, an amazing girlfriend and I know you are going to be an amazing wife and mother to our children," he said.

I was crying but my heart was beating fast too, because I knew what was going to happen next.

"Chahat Aggarwal, will you do the honour of changing your surname to Chahat Aryan Kapoor? Will you be the mother to our children? Will you marry me? Will you be mine forever?" he asked and opened the box, making me look at the big, shining and absolutely gorgeous solitaire ring in it.

I cried harder and couldn't utter a word. I was speechless. I tried to find my voice, but no words came out, so I nodded excitedly.

He smiled and that's probably the biggest smile I had ever seen on his face. He asked for my hand and I happily gave it to him.

He put his ring on my ring finger and got up. I hugged him tightly as I cried and kissed him with so much love. I felt his tears on my face too and our tears made our kiss more special.

"I love you, soon to be Mrs Kapoor." He muttered as we pulled away.

"I love you too Mr Kapoor," I said, smiling.

After Aryan proposed, we had an amazing dinner.

"You've made me the happiest person alive," he said as we were back in his car.

"No. It's you who have made me the happiest girl alive. When did you plan all this, by the way?" I asked.

"After we returned. My parents, your parents and all our friends helped me plan it all," he said, as our hands intertwined.

"You guys are amazing. I just love you all," I said as I made a mental note to thank everyone.

"I love you too, baby. Do you want to spend the night together?" he asked.

"Your parents?" I asked.

"They are not here. They left yesterday for Delhi. They'll come back tomorrow," He said.

"Oh nice! Even my parents…" he cut me off.

"I know. They are in America. They told me," he said, smirking.

I laughed and nodded. We went to his place and he gave me his tee and shorts to change into. I changed, but those shorts were falling to the floor again and again, so I decided not to wear them. That tall man's tee was reaching my mid-thighs, anyway.

I got out of his big washroom and spotted Aryan with nothing but only his shorts on. I went towards him and he looked at me with his eyes roaming all over my body.

"You're hot," he muttered suddenly. "But you look hotter when you wear my tee," he added.

I gave him a naughty look.

"Well, you haven't seen my fiancé then. He's the hottest guy ever," I said as I got on the bed with him and laid down beside him.

"Aha?" he asked, as suddenly he got on top of me.

I nodded as I put my arms around his neck. We started kissing each other passionately. Our lips moved perfectly against each other's lips. They knew no separation. His hands kept moving all over my body while my hands moved on his back, my nails leaving marks on his back.

We slowly pulled away as we were breathless, but this time, we didn't stop. We weren't in our senses. He got rid of my tee and left me in nothing but my inner wear. I felt vulnerable and naked under his gaze.

"You are so freaking beautiful, my angel," he said, looking in my eyes and his words made me feel more beautiful than I had ever felt.

I blushed and looked away, but he held my chin as he kissed my forehead, then my nose, my lips, my jaw and then went down to my neck. He kissed my neck and that kiss made me feel a new kind of sensation down there.

He was making me feel something new!

He continued kissing and licking it before moving to my shoulder and doing the same there.

"We can stop if you want," he said with darkened eyes.

"No! I am ready, really. I love you Aryan, so much that I am ready to take a step further with you, my forever one," I said, breathless.

He claimed my lips and kissed me passionately before we undressed each other and made love for the first time.

The next morning, I woke up with Aryan's arm around me.

I turned around and blushed as I remembered our last night together.

I looked at him, and even for a second, I didn't regret what we had done. I finally gave myself to the guy who loved me and treated me with utmost respect. It was beyond beautiful. Although it was a totally different and new experience, he made it worth everything.

"Good morning, my beautiful fiancé," he said, smiling.

"Good morning to you too, my love," I said smiling.

We stayed in the bed for some more time before we went down and had breakfast.

He had an important meeting, so he went there, while I went home. Samaira and I had decided to meet that day. After catching up over a cup of coffee, I came back and finished the painting I have been working on.

The next few weeks passed in a blur as I was with Samaira the entire time. Samaira had got engaged to Siddhant and it was almost like a beautiful dream turning into reality. I didn't miss happiness in Siddhant's eyes as he saw her. Just as I wished, she had an amazing love story.

The next few days, I was painting again as my paintings were in demand these days. One day, I was painting when the bell rang. I opened the door, and to my shock, there was Samaira, with tears in her eyes.

"Samaira, what's up? Come inside," I said, and she hugged me tightly, crying inconsolably.

I was beyond worried. I got her inside and rubbed her back before I gave her water. She cried her heart out and I didn't leave her side. She calmed down after a bit and I asked her what happened.

She told me that she had called off the engagement.

I was again beyond shocked when I heard that. They loved each other, they were each other's lifeline. What happened to make them take this step?

She started telling me everything – from her feeling bad, to her dreams, to calling her engagement and a beautiful relationship off. She also told me about Siddhant's changed behaviour and about his friend Tia.

"He gave so much importance to her. It hurt me. How could he? 'Just a mere friend.' His line is still echoing in my mind. How can he act like nothing happened? Didn't he love me? I can't stop my tears right now and he must be 'catching up' with his Tia," she said, crying as she was done telling me about what had happened.

"What a bastard!" I said as I hugged her.

We talked for a long time and she decided to stay for the night. I was with her the entire day and I tried to cheer her up. We watched a comedy movie that made her smile, after a long time. We slept in my room that night.

Aryan was there the next day as usual and I told him everything before he said he would talk to Siddhant.

I also made Samaira her favourite pancakes and we went on a girls' day out. We shopped before Samaira met Tia in the mall and we had to come back home. That night Aryan took both of us to dinner in a nice restaurant. The next day, Samaira went back home, even though I asked her to stay. At least I was glad that she was better than before. I was very sad that even after being engaged and being so much in love, they had failed to have a happily ever after together.

How I wish destiny would be on my best friend's side and let her be with the one she loved deeply!

~

I was painting one night when I got a call from Aryan.

"Hi babe," I said, smiling.

"Hi," he said, sounding very low.

"What's up?" I asked, all attentive.

"I'm on my way to your place. We have to go to the hospital," he said.

"Why? What's wrong? Is everyone okay?" I asked, getting up.

"Samaira met with an accident. She's saved, but she's in coma," Aryan said and I felt my world getting hit by a tornado.

My paintbrush fell from my hand as tears fell from my eyes.

"What?" I shouted.

"Say it's a lie," I continued, crying.

"Babe, I wish. I am here. Come now. I don't want you crying alone," he said and I know he was feeling my pain.

I quickly went down and locked the door. I sat in Aryan's car and he hugged me tightly.

"I'm right here," he said, as he hugged me and I couldn't help but cry.

I pulled away and we started for the hospital. We reached and met Samaira and Siddhant's family there. I sat with Samaira's mother as she cried.

We stayed for a while before it was very late and we had to leave. That night, Aryan stayed with me at my place and hugged me while I cried myself to sleep.

∾

It had been a week since Samaira was in coma and I made sure to visit her every day. I was really worried about her and I had no idea when she would wake up.

I was on my way to the hospital when I got a call from Samaira's mother.

"Hello?" I said.

"Samaira has woken up!" she said excitedly.

"Oh my god! That's amazing! I'll be there soon," I said.

I was so happy!

I reached the hospital and met her. She tried smiling at me and I was about to cry. I then went near her and held her free hand in mine. We talked for a while, before it was time for her to rest. I kissed her forehead and left.

I was so happy and relieved after that! Soon, she'll be all right, I told myself.

I went directly to Aryan's office. I stayed with Aryan and was extremely excited while I told him that Samaira had revived and would be fine in a few days. He sat there, smiling throughout while he watched me talk. I even wondered in between whether he was actually listening. I stopped to be sure, but when I stopped, he would tell me to continue.

A month passed and Samaira and Siddhant were together again after their drastic break up. They managed to be together even after such huge differences, lies and tears. It wasn't less than any miracle! It was a terrible time for both of them. They were now going to get married after a months' time in Mumbai and I was really excited about that. I had already spent some sleepless nights to finish off all my paintings so that I could be with Samaira while she prepared for her wedding.

Mom and Dad had returned from America some time back and had left for Europe for a business conference. They were to come back just two weeks before Samaira's wedding. Also, my parents were extremely ecstatic when they saw the big diamond ring on my finger and were very excited to learn that Aryan was going to be their son-in-law.

∾

Aryan was with me in my room, lying on my bed while I twirled in front of him in my golden dress that I was going to wear in one of the functions before Samaira's wedding.

"You look amazing," Aryan said.

"I like this dress," I said.

"Me too, but I know I'm going to love your wedding dress the most when you'll be walking towards me to get married," he said, smiling.

I blushed.

"I was thinking it's time. Today when uncle and aunty will be back, we can talk to them about our wedding," Aryan said.

"Yes. I guess it's time," I said, smiling.

"I love you so much!" he said as he smiled at me.

"I love you too," I said, honestly. My feelings for him had never changed in the past years and I was sure that they never even would.

My life was perfect!

"When are they reaching, by the way?" he asked.

"Their flight has landed. They'll be here anytime now. They have been gone for so long and I miss them. I can't wait to see them again," I said, and just then my phone rang.

"Hello?" I said as I picked up the call.

"Miss Aggarwal?" Someone asked.

"Yes, that's me. How can I help you?" I asked as I looked at myself through the mirror.

"I found your number from this person's phone. You were the last person she dialled, so that's why I called you," The person said.

"Who? Mom?" I asked, confused.

By now, Aryan was looking at me and raising his eyebrow and I shrugged to that.

"Probably. I am really sorry to tell you that two people, probably your parents, have met with an accident. The accident was so severe that they couldn't make it." he said.

My phone fell from my hands as I heard those words. My world collapsed. My parents were no more! They met with an accident. The two people who brought me into this world had now left this world. How could they do this? They have to come! They have to! They can't go!

I loved them the most! I trusted them the most! They were the ones who held my little hands and taught me how to walk. They stayed up with me when I couldn't sleep. They worked hard so that I got a comfortable life. They sacrificed their big joys so that I could have my little joys!

They laughed when they saw me laughing, they cried when they saw me crying, they smiled when they saw me smiling, but the harsh, bitter reality now was that they won't see me anymore. They won't hear me now. They can't hug me. They can't bless me.

I felt Aryan picking the phone and handling me. He hugged me tightly after he talked to that person. He said some soothing words in my ears, but I didn't hear anything.

Home was never going to be the same without them. Screw that! Home will not be home. It'll be a mere house. No feeling, no warmth, no laughter. Completely empty.

My world was never going to be the same without them in it.

How can the world be so cruel! How can destiny be so cruel to me! What did I do wrong that my brother was taken away and then my parents left me all alone?

'Who was that insensitive person who hit my parent's car and fled?'

'I can't forgive that person ever!'

'He's a murderer! He's cruel! He's not a human, he has taken away two lives! He's a monster! He's a criminal and this world has no place for such criminals!'

'Why? Why my parents, you monster? Why?'

∾

After the funeral was over the next day, everyone went back home. Samaira and Siddhant were even willing to postpone their wedding, but I stopped them. It would make things difficult for them as all the preparations were already done. Everyone had been extremely helpful to me in these difficult times. Yesterday, Aryan and I had spent the night together at his place. I cried the entire night in Aryan's arms. Uncle and aunty were very nice and comforted me a lot.

There was emptiness in me which nothing in the world could fill.

∾

Two weeks passed and I came face to face with the reality. I was thankful to god for Aryan as he never left my side. If he was not by my side, I don't know whether I would even be able to breathe.

That day, one of Samaira's wedding functions was being held at a hotel and we had to be there. I was ready while Aryan was still in the shower. I went to the living room and stood in front of my parents' picture, which now had a garland around it.

"Mom, Dad. You are not here anymore. I am feeling lonely and want to cry again, and keep crying. But you are not there to wipe my tears and say I am your strong girl and that I don't have to cry. When I used to cry, you both wiped my tears. You always used to tell me there isn't a thing that has no solution, but there is such a thing. Your death has no solution. I was waiting for you both to come back home to me. I thought my life was perfect, but just then, you left. You left me to fight this cruel world alone," I said as I couldn't help but cry.

"You both have been the best parents and your guidance has always worked. Mom's clever talks and Dad's jokes made this house, a home. Whenever I came back, mom's yummy food's aroma would fill my nostrils, but there won't be anything of that sort now," I stopped as I hiccupped.

"Mom, Dad, this loss can't be fixed, but you'll always be in my heart. You'll be in my prayers. I have to move on, but wherever life takes me, I'll take you both along. I love you both so much, always. Always be happy and keep looking at me from heaven. I know now that you are there; you will make sure that god blesses me with enough strength to deal with this loss," I said and felt a bit strong having vented all that out.

"And I'll make sure Aryan and my children know every bit of their grandparents. Aryan has helped me a lot in coping up with this time. I am so blessed to have him," I said and I felt a presence behind me when I stopped.

I turned and spotted Aryan, ready for the function.

"Hi Mom, Dad. Your daughter is very strong. Probably, the strongest. You have raised her in the most amazing manner. I know you are looking at her from heaven and are always so proud of her. Today, I, Aryan, am here to ask for her hand. I love her and I promise I am going to keep her safe, happy and smiling always," he said and I fell in love with him all over again.

I hugged him and he hugged me back.

"My strong lady," he said and then we both left for the function.

The wedding was the next day and I was excited to see my best friend as a bride.

"Darling! Let's go. We are getting late," Aryan said.

"Yes love," I responded.

We smiled and left for Samaira's wedding function.

Soon, Samaira and Siddhant became a married couple and we bid them goodbye. That night, Aryan and I slept together somewhat at peace.

But then, I got a call.

Aryan

December 2014

I came out of my thoughts when I heard a knock on the door. I told the person to come in.

"Sir, we can't track Ms Aggarwal," one of my trusted men said.

"Send some men to look for her at the airport, railway station, bus stops and every possible transport," I ordered and they nodded before they left.

"I'll just visit her place, maybe she is back at her place," I said as I got up and left for her home.

I was stressed the whole time. Maybe I was just overthinking. She must be having a bad day and missing her parents and just wanted to be alone at home and paint.

The driver stopped in front of her home for the second time that day and I went in. Everything was still and in place, like I had left it. I entered her room and found everything just the same. Her paintings were kept in a corner. I could say that no one had been there after I had left. I didn't lose hope and went to the park to find her, but all in vain. I even went and checked the place I used as my escape. She loved it too, as from there we could see the entire city. But she wasn't there as well.

I called Samaira who was now in UAE. I told her everything. She promised she was going to try calling Chahat and also ask everyone she thought could help.

Just as I entered my office, I got a call from Samaira.

"Were you able to find anything?" I asked.

"I'm so sorry Aryan, but no one knows where Chahat is. I tried calling her too, but her number isn't reachable," she said and by her voice, I could tell she was worried for Chahat.

"I just hope she's safe and comes back home as soon as possible," I said and sighed.

"I'll just call her parents—" She didn't complete the sentence when she remembered that Chahat's parents were no longer alive.

"I'm sorry," she muttered and sighed.

"No problem. Samaira, you be with Siddhant! I'll find her. Don't worry and I'll call you when I come to know about her whereabouts," I said.

Soon, Siddhant and Abhi called me and I told them everything. They were ready to come to be with me and help find her. I declined because Siddhant had to leave for his honeymoon and Abhi had to be with Kaira as she was pregnant.

I told my parents too and dad started to call every person who could help me find her. The night came and it was almost an entire day since Chahat left.

There was no trace of her. No one knew where she was. She just disappeared. I didn't even know whether she was in Mumbai.

The night passed and I hoped she would come the next day.

The next day passed, and just like that, a week passed, but nothing happened.

Now everyone had started to believe that she was gone. Gone forever!

That night, I went to my room and locked myself. I couldn't control my emotions anymore, so I simply broke down. I gave up.

I leaned back on the door as tears fell from my eyes. I slid down by the door and sat on the floor. There was no stopping my tears.

"I can't live without you." The words unknowingly left my mouth.

My heart was broken; it was aching. There was a constant pain in my chest that was not letting me do anything.

"Chahat, you are the best thing that had ever happened to me. Your smile, your laugh, your sarcasm... everything is still so fresh in my mind. I can't believe you are gone. You didn't even think about what would happen to me after you're gone! I had dreams of a true love and you came and made me feel it, experience it, but you didn't live it with me. When it was time to be each other's forever, you left. Was it so difficult to wake me up when you got a call?" A sob left my mouth, but I continued as I let all my feelings, questions and tears out.

"I never thought I'd cry. I never thought I'd care for a girl so much. I never thought I'd plan so many special dates and surprises for a girl. When you came, I changed. The moronic Aryan changed into a new Aryan, who was passionate, hard working and a one-woman man. I wanted to have a bright future with you. I don't know how I am going to live. You have made a hole in my heart, Chahat," I kept saying and crying as I felt alone, lonely and heartbroken.

"I have no idea where you are. I have no idea whether you are even breathing or you have given up your life. Chahat, I don't know why destiny is doing this to us. I don't know why this is happening to us. Why?

"One thing is for sure Chahat. If not you, then no one. No one can take your place in my life. I can't give my heart to anyone else, because your name is written on this heart for eternity. I won't be able to give myself to anyone else."

"I was so happy when you asked for my opinions in all your decisions. I was so happy when I was the one who held you in my arms when you were crying. I was so happy when I was the first one you called when you had some good news to share. You made me feel important! How I want to take away all your pain, all your grief and bring you back! How I want to fight for you, but I can't, because I don't know what to do. I don't know anything, but the one thing I do know is that I may not be near you or know anything about you, but I will always be the one who is praying for your success and health. I may lose all my trust in god, but I'll still pray only for you. I may lose all the will to live, but I'll still live so that I can relive the memories I have with you. I promise you this," I said as I kept crying.

"I love you. I won't stop loving you. Ever. No matter how many generations pass. No matter what Chahat, no matter what. This heart is only yours. This body is only yours. This life is only yours. I may live, but I won't be alive. I may breathe, but it won't have any meaning. Please come back, Chahat. I beg you. I am ready to take away all your pain and solve every problem you are fighting, but please come back to me!" I said as I cried harder.

Aryan

April 2019

"Sir, the files are ready," my assistant said.

I nodded and after reading them, I signed them. My assistant left my office. I moved towards the glass window in my office and looked out of it. I had a glass of whiskey in my hand.

I took a sip, standing in one of the most successful business companies. In the last five years, I had spent most of my time in my office, working and occasionally drinking along. My hard work had got the company to reach heights of success. My parents were proud of me for it, but they didn't like my being a workaholic. They wanted me to hang out with my friends, fall in love, marry and have kids. If only they knew it wasn't so easy.

It still felt like it was yesterday that Chahat left. No one knew where she was. No one knew how she was. No one knew whether she was even alive.

There was a knock on the door and in walked my parents.

"Hey son," they said, almost in unison.

"Hey Mom, Dad!" I said as I kept aside my glass and sat down on my chair.

They looked at the glass and sighed. They did not like my drinking even occasionally, especially because I never drank before Chahat left.

"Aryan, it's been five years since she has gone. She is never going to come back. We have done everything we could to find her, but seems like she either herself isn't willing to come back or she can't come back because she's no more. It's time you move on," Mom started.

"We have had this conversation many times," I said.

"Son, we aren't getting any younger. Before we leave this earth, we want you in good hands. We will die in peace only when we know that there's someone who will take care of Aryan after us," Dad said.

"Nothing is happening to you, Dad. Not now, not ever," I said.

"Aryan, please! It's not the time for all this. For our sake, you have to move on!" Mom said.

"Yes son! You have to move on," Dad said.

What was wrong with them? Suddenly it made sense.

"Who is she?" I asked.

"Who?" Mom asked, acting clueless.

"The girl you think is suitable for me. I know you both too well. You already have a girl in mind and that's why you are here to convince me," I said.

They looked at each other and Dad nodded at Mom.

"Her name is Kajal Pathania. She's the daughter of a big businessman in America. She's a very beautiful girl and intelligent too. She works with her father. Her father likes you very much. We both like her too. It'll be best if you go to America and see her," Mom said.

"Actually—" I started but Mom cut me off.

"Aryan, I am not telling you to forget Chahat. Keep her in your heart. You know if she was here then she would have wanted your happiness. I loved her and I still love her. She would have been the best daughter-in-law. We'll keep her alive in our lives with the beautiful memories she has given us. Seeing you drink would make her sad, but seeing you happy, even with another girl, would make her smile. Love is like that, my son. Love is pure and love is happiness. Aryan, keep Chahat in your heart, but also open your heart to other things at the same time. Keep Chahat safe in your memories, but also make new memories. Keep Chahat alive in you, but you also have to keep yourself alive," Mom said.

I listened to her as I tried to stop the tear that was threatening to fall. My hand moved towards the glass of whiskey when I was about to cry, but this time, I stopped as mom's words rang in my head again.

'Seeing you drinking would make her sad.'

I called my assistant.

"Please send someone to take away the liquor bottle from my office," I said and hung up.

Mom and Dad smiled at me. A sadly happy smile.

"Son, we are very happy that you made an effort to quit drinking. I am proud of you, like always. Now, I hope you are going to make us and Chahat happy by being happy yourself. I hope you will take your decision as soon as possible," Dad said as my office door opened and Abhi and Siddhant entered.

Abhi and Siddhant have been busy with their work and their family as now both of them were fathers to cute little kids, but they were the best ever friends. They have been with me whenever I needed someone. They always motivate me and it was only because of them that I had managed to even smile in the past few years.

"Did we miss something?" Abhi asked as they took a seat with Mom and Dad.

"Oh yes!" Dad answered.

"Aryan, we know it's difficult, but give it a try, man. It's breaking both of us to see you like this," Siddhant said.

"Yes man! It is! We want our old Aryan back. We all want him! Chahat wants it! Why can't you give him back to us?" Abhi said.

There was a two-minute silence before I started.

"It's not easy for you all to look at me working all day, drinking and never laughing. I know it's very hard. I know how much it affects you all. I, only for you four and my Chahat, will meet Kajal," I said as I took a deep breath.

All of their faces broke into a grins as they got up and hugged me tight.

"You have made me so happy today," Mom said as she hugged me tight.

I smiled at her and hoped what I had decided was for good.

∾

"Hello, Mr Kapoor. This is my daughter, Kajal," Mr Pathania introduced us.

"Hey. I'm Aryan Kapoor. Glad to meet you both," I said.

It had been a week since I said yes to meeting Kajal, and they were here. Kajal arrived with her father from America to see me.

Kajal was really cute and beautiful. She had pretty eyes and a perfect nose. She was also tall, quite unlike Chahat.

"It's so good to finally meet your daughter. She is actually very beautiful," Mom said.

"Thank you!" Kajal replied, smiling.

"Well, you both go and talk before we decide anything," Dad said and Kajal and I left for a garden that was located here in the resort.

"Hey," she said.

"Hey," I said before the situation turned awkward.

"So, were you forced into this?" she asked as we were walking.

"Kind of, but I think it's time and their push was needed, so I guess I am cool," I said.

"Me too. I feel it's time for me to settle down," she said.

"How come you're single?" I asked, confused.

"I didn't get you," she said.

"I mean, you are beautiful, successful, talented and rich. How are you single?" I asked.

"Well, I believed in true love. Yes, I had a few relationships in the past, but I called it off when I knew it wasn't for me. What about you?" she asked.

"That's good. Me? Well, one serious relationship, but it didn't end on good terms, so here I am," I said.

"I'm so sorry," she said.

"No, no. That's totally cool," I said.

And then we went on about our careers, dreams and choices. It was good to talk to someone after so long. After we went back inside, my parents looked at me hopefully. After having our lunch, we all left the resort.

"So, how was it?" Mom asked once we reached home.

"It was good," I replied.

"So? What's your decision?" Mom asked.

"I guess I can look forward to the next meeting," I said, as I thought of having a good talking session with her next time.

"Oh my god! That's amazing," Mom said happily.

"I'll give Mr Pathania a call immediately," Dad said, getting up.

What? I didn't mean that!

"Mom, Dad! I didn't mean that! I meant that I can look forward to meet her the next time but that doesn't mean I'll marry her too," I said.

"Oh! Don't worry! Meet her again and I know you will eventually marry her and bring Kajal home," Mom said, excitedly.

"I called Mr Pathania. Some important work has come up and Kajal has to return tomorrow, but why don't you go to America and meet her?" Dad asked.

"I have to go to America for a meeting next week. I guess I'll see her then," I said.

"Amazing! See, even destiny is with you. Right honey? After all, it's destiny that after seeing Kajal today, he has a meeting in America the next week, so that he can meet his future wife once again!" Mom said.

Mom will be Mom! Destiny? It was the most terrible thing. Well, in my case it had been destiny that stole away the girl I had loved with all my heart.

Dad nodded, smiling, before I shook my head at them and went to my room.

I entered my room and saw Chahat's photo that I had kept in my room.

"I miss you so much," I whispered as I looked at her big grin in the picture.

I lay down on my bed and I knew Kajal was going to be an amazing friend, if not wife. She's amazing, but I don't get the same feeling with her that I got with Chahat.

Chahat was someone else! Someone I just can't find again! Who was a single model made by god. I smiled at the thought before calling it a day.

The whole week passed in a blur, and soon, I was in America. I went to my hotel and slept as I had a terrible jet lag. The next day, I got ready and attended the meeting I was travelling for.

"So, I firmly believe that this deal will be beneficial for both of us," I said as I finished the presentation.

"We absolutely loved the idea, Mr Kapoor, but we still need some time before we finalise the deal to analyse the resources and all the budget required. We hope you and your team don't mind," Mr Collins said.

"That won't be a problem. You can have all the time you want, but it would be really great if you inform us in two days," I said.

"We can definitely assure you on that, Mr Kapoor," Mr Collins said, as he got up and we shook hands.

I left the conference room and sat in my car when my phone buzzed.

Kajal: *Hi Aryan! I hope you are done with your meetings.*
Aryan: *Hi. I just finished with the meetings.*
Kajal: *Great! How about lunch together?*
Aryan: *Alright. Where to?*
Kajal: *Come to my office. We can leave together.*

I replied with an okay and she sent me the address. I gave the driver the address and he drove me to Kajal's office. We reached her office and the receptionist guided me to her cabin. I knocked and went in to find her working.

"Oh hi! I am done. Just a moment," she said, getting up.

"Take your time," I said as my eyes roamed around her office. Her office was simple, but elegant.

"Let's go," she said, as she took her bag.

I nodded and we moved out of her office room.

"So, how was your flight?" Kajal asked as we walked to the elevator.

"It was..." I was interrupted by the situation that happened in the next few seconds.

The elevator dinged and opened slowly.

My eyes drifted to the now opened elevator as I was speaking, when I got the greatest shock of my life.

My eyes fell on the face that I had craved to find for the past five years! My eyes fell on the smile that I had missed seeing for the past five years!

Chahat's face came in front of me and she looked at Kajal smiling, before she looked at me, and I knew the shock was mutual. Her smile faded and her eyes opened wide. Her eyes were different now than they were five years before. Her eyes now had a mystery, a secret behind.

"Oh! Aryan, this is my friend and assistant, Ayushi. Ayushi, this is my friend from Mumbai, Aryan Kapoor," Kajal introduced.

What? Ayushi?

She's not Ayushi! She can't be Ayushi, because she's Chahat!

Chahat overcame the shock and tried to smile at me, although I knew it wasn't her smile. It was a fake one. She had different emotions right now. She had different feelings right now. And all of it just didn't let her smile.

"Hi," she stammered.

It felt like eternity since I had heard her voice.

Her voice was still fresh in my head and in her memories, but listening to it again was causing me to break down.

As I looked at her face again, I couldn't help but feel emotional. I was about to break down, my tears were on the verge on falling. I wanted to question her as to why she had run away like that. Why did she never come back? All these years, I have been waiting for her, struggling to find the will to live, and she has been in America making new friends! Why?

I missed her, I cried for her, I begged god to bring her back and here she was, having a new life, having new friends. And to top it all, having a new name.

I knew her! Too well, or maybe I just thought I did!

I felt Kajal placing her hand on my forearm, probably because I had been lost in my thoughts for too long.

Chahat's eyes followed Kajal's hand that was on my forearm and I did see a change in the expression on her face.

'Some things never change!' I thought as I noticed the jealousy and possessiveness on Chahat's face. I smiled.

"Hi," I said with my voice cold. I don't know why and how it came out like that.

"Ayushi, please check my desk for that document I mentioned earlier. I had kept it on my desk," Kajal said.

"Sure," Chahat said.

"Also, now that your lunch is done, after leaving the documents at the reception, come back and open the box on the right side of my desk and you'll find some files in it. Arrange them all alphabetically and I'll be back by then," Kajal ordered.

"Okay. I'll just get to it," Chahat said and she tried to look at me, but for some reason, her eyes were stuck to the floor. She couldn't look at me in the eyes. She just moved by Kajal's side and entered Kajal's office.

"Come on," Kajal said and we entered the elevator.

I didn't say a word. I was too confused, shocked and silent. I just saw Chahat after five years. She was a different person! She had a different personality. She wasn't the Chahat I knew.

But the most shocking thing was that Chahat was Kajal's secretary. Chahat never wanted a job like that. She had said she would take up such a job when she would lose the will to live... to feel alive.

Her words were still fresh in my mind like it was yesterday.

So, can it be? Has she quit the idea of feeling alive? Is she not interested in living anymore? Is she living just for the sake of living and not because she wants to live and feel the moment?

"Aryan?" Kajal called.

"Oh yes?" I said, as I came out of my trance.

"We have reached," Kajal said.

We entered the hotel and had a good lunch. We talked, but I couldn't focus as my mind was busy thinking about the girl who was the only girl I have loved and whom I had met after five long years.

After lunch, Kajal and I sat back in my car and left for her office.

"So, that was your secretary?" I asked as I was dying to know that.

"Yes. Ayushi is my secretary, but a friend too. That's why we are on first name basis," Kajal said.

"Okay. So, is she new?" I asked.

"Not really. Since four years or so. She had been my friend for almost a year before she joined the company," Kajal replied and just then her phone rang.

"Yes Ayushi?" Kajal asked.

My heart began to beat faster! But her number never existed whenever I called.

'As if she couldn't get a new one!' *My inner voice reminded.*

"Oh! What's wrong?" Kajal asked, suddenly worried.

For some reason, I also got worried. Is Chahat okay? Is she not well? What happened?

"You go back home. I'm on my way anyway," Kajal said and hung up later.

"What's wrong?" I asked.

"Ayushi's father isn't well," Kajal said as she kept her phone in her bag.

What?

"Her father?" I asked Kajal.

"Yes. Her father isn't well. Maybe I'll go and see him too," she said and just then we reached her office.

"It was really great to have lunch with you! See you soon," She said and got out of the car.

After she left, I sat confused and I tried to put everything in place.

First, meeting Chahat suddenly after five long years.

Second, her name changed to Ayushi.

Thirdly, her working in a 9 to 5 job which she never wanted.

And now, her father was alive!

But her father was dead; her mother was dead as well. I was there at their funeral. It all happened in front of my eyes.

Had her father faked his death?

But why?

I closed my eyes.

"I need my answers," I whispered to myself, determined.

After I reached my suite, I immediately called Siddhant and Abhi.

"Hey Aryan. What's up?" Siddhant said.

"Hi Siddhant. Abhi is here too," I said.

"Hey guys. What's up, Aryan?" Abhi said.

"Guys, I met Chahat," I said.

"What?" They both said at the same time.

And then I explained everything to them, how I met her, how her name was changed and how her father was still alive.

"That's impossible! Her parents died years back! Her name is changed! She is in America! I just can't understand what's going on. Aryan, are you sure she was Chahat?" Abhi asked.

"Hundred percent. There's no one who could identify her better than me. It was her," I said.

"Listen, I have some sources in America. I'll tell them to enquire about Chahat. I mean, Ayushi," Siddhant said.

"That'll be great," I said.

After I talked to them, I was still lost in Chahat. Her voice, her face, her smile, her eyes filled with jealousy, her hair, her sad eyes – it was all coming back to my mind again and again.

Why couldn't I take her in my arms? Why couldn't I tell her how much I missed her? Why couldn't I tell her that I still loved her and how I had been when she was gone? Why couldn't I ask her where she had been all these years and why she had left?

Siddhant's call brought me back from my thoughts.

"Hi. Did you find anything?" I asked.

"Hi. I called my men and they'll enquire about Chahat and give us the details by day after tomorrow," Siddhant said.

"Can't I get it by tomorrow?" I asked.

"No. I am afraid that it is the earliest," Siddhant said.

"Oh! That's okay. Thank you so much," I said.

"Shut up, man! Chill and don't worry. If destiny has it, Chahat and you will be back together," Siddhant said.

"I wish, but I need my answers," I said.

"You have got all the rights to have them," Siddhant said.

We hung up, but I just couldn't wait until day after. Soon, my eyes shut and sleep consumed me. I woke up around dinner time and saw a missed call from mom.

"Hey Mom," I said.

"How is she?" Mom said.

"Kajal is fine," I said. I knew who she was referring to, but for some reason I didn't want to talk about it.

"I am asking about Chahat. How is she?" she asked.

"She is supposed to be good," I said, curtly.

"I see, you didn't like the changes you witnessed in her," Mom said.

"I don't know. I saw her after so many years. I don't know what's going on and what is going to happen next. I don't know what destiny has for me next. I don't know, Mom," I said.

"Hey, Aryan! That's okay! That's totally fine! My child, don't worry. If she loved you, if her love was true, then even this entire world and the worst situations of life will be nothing in front of her love," Mom said and I felt relieved.

Sometimes, just a few words by your Mom can be enough to calm the chaos inside you.

I talked to her for a bit more and disconnected her call as Mr Pathania was calling me.

"Hello Mr Pathania," I said.

"My child, you are welcome to call me uncle," he said.

"Yes, uncle," I said.

"That's more like it. I hope you haven't had your dinner, because for all the nights you are spending in America, you just can't have the hotel's cuisine," he said.

"No, I haven't had my dinner yet," I replied.

"Amazing. I'll send the driver to get you home. It would be a pleasure to have you here," He said.

"No, no—" He cut me off.

"I am not taking that for an answer, dear. Come soon," he said and after I reluctantly agreed, we hung up.

I got ready before I was informed that the driver was there. I moved down and sat in the car. I looked out of the window and I knew that Chahat and I were under the same sky and maybe not even a mile away. The thought was giving me a different feeling. I wanted to run, I wanted to look for her, I wanted to see her again and keep her safe this time.

Kajal's home was a big mansion with a beautiful interior and exterior.

I was engulfed in a hug by Kajal's mom and a side hug by her father. I met Kajal again and she smiled sweetly at me.

"He's so handsome and looks so much more sincere in person," her mom complimented.

"Thank you," I said, before we all shifted to the dining room.

"So, how's business?" Uncle asked.

"It's going great," I replied.

"How are your parents? I was looking forward to meeting them," Aunty said.

"They are great. Even they were keen, but I guess you'll meet them soon," I said and I played my words again in my mind and I realised that I was giving a hint that I was planning to marry Kajal.

"I hope so. Anyway, this reminds me, Kajal, how is Naresh?" Uncle asked.

"He's good dad. Just an upset stomach. Nothing major," Kajal replied before taking a bite from her spaghetti.

"That's good. I talked to Deepika too. Did you go and meet him?" Aunty asked.

"Yes. I went to see him after lunch. Deepika aunty was worried and the doctor was there. The doctor concluded it was just some stomach infection. Deepika aunty was scolding him later," Kajal said and chuckled.

"This couple is one in a million," Aunty said, smiling and we all continued eating and making a small talk in between.

Naresh? Kajal went to see Chahat's father, but as far as I remember, Naresh wasn't the name of her father. And Deepika? Her mother's name was Seema. Did they also change their names?

Who are they? Are they really Chahat's parents?

Later that night, I left their home for my hotel.

I knew I needed my answers, and I was going to have them soon.

Aryan

The next day, I got up around 8 in the morning. Although I had slept around 5, for all my sleep was taken away by Chahat's thoughts.

I went for a jog and after coming back at around 10, I got ready in a casual attire and had my breakfast in the hotel's restaurant. I went back to my room and changed into my suit. I sat in the car and told the driver to start for Kajal's office. I had to reach her office and meet Chahat. No matter what, I was going to have my answers.

Just on the way, I got a call.

"Hello, Mr Collins," I said as I picked up the call.

"Hello, Mr Kapoor. I am glad to tell you that the deal is finalised between us," he said.

"That's amazing. Thank you so much," I said, happily.

"You're welcome. It's an amazing opportunity for us. I would like to inform you that I have to leave for Europe today evening. Sorry to inform you on such a short notice, but can you come and sign the contract now and complete the formalities?" he said.

"Actually, I had plans. I can meet you after two hours," I said.

"I am afraid, I won't be here by then. I'll return only after a month and I feel it won't be really convenient for you and for us to wait for that long," he said.

"All right then! I'll be there," I said. I'll meet Chahat after signing, I told myself.

We hung up and I told the driver to reroute towards Mr Collins' office. I closed my eyes and sighed loudly.

I reached there in no time and met Mr Collins. I read the contract and signed it. It was a good thing that he had a flight, otherwise it would have taken me hours there with him. I left his office and started for Kajal's office.

I got a call from an unknown number while I was on the way.

"Hello, am I speaking to Mr Aryan?" The person said on the other side.

"Yes. Who is it?" I asked, rubbing my forehead.

"I am David. Mr Siddhant asked me to enquire about Ms Ayushi and let you know," he said.

This was it!

"Yes. So, what did you find and you were to inform me by tomorrow…?" I asked, curiously.

"There wasn't much information about her, so it didn't take me much time to find out," he said.

"Okay, what did you find?" I asked.

"I can give you the whole document in person. Where can you meet me?" he asked.

"I am on my way to somewhere. Will it be okay if you mail me the photo of it right now?" I asked and silently prayed that it was possible.

"Of course. I'll leave the copy at your hotel reception and send you the picture of it now," he said and I thanked him before we hung up.

I got the mail in a minute and I downloaded it right away.

Name	:	*Ayushi Chawla*
Parents	:	*Naresh Chawla* *Deepika Chawla*
Status	:	*Single*
Age	:	*29 (turning 30 in two months)*
Sibling	:	*None.*
Best friend	:	*Kajal Pathania*
Work	:	*Assistant of Kajal Pathania*
School	:	*Private education.*
College	:	*Private education.*
Nationality	:	*Parents are Indian but she is born, raised and lived all her life in America.*

What the hell! Her parents were dead. She has lived all her life in India. Her education wasn't private! Her college wasn't private! She had a sibling!

I could easily say that the information was fake. It was all made up. I know that! But why? Why did she make a fake identity?

'Now only she has the answers to this.' I thought, determined.

I reached Kajal's office building and went straight to Kajal's floor. I was sure Chahat's office would be on that floor only. I spotted Kajal's cabin's door and the other door, comparatively smaller than that of Kajal's, and I knew it was the one to Chahat's office. I knocked and I heard a come in. Her voice giving me chills and making me lose all the confidence with which I walked in. I walked into her office and she was sitting there, typing on the computer.

"Yes?" she said, without looking at me.

"I need my answers," I said and her eyes widened before she looked at me immediately. Her mouth was slightly open and she slowly got up from her seat.

"Aryan," she whispered as she was now standing, with teary eyes, an open mouth and her hands gripping her table as if to keep her stable.

"Chahat," I said and her eyes blinked as if she had heard it after years.

"Why?" I continued and a tear dropped from her eyes as her eyes were fixed on my face. Her eyes made me feel vulnerable. Her gaze was so strong, like she was trying to remember each detail of my face.

A tear fell from my eyes as I looked at her face. Her face was the same as before. Same eyes, the same smile, same looks, same hair. How much had I missed it all!

Suddenly she took a breath and regained her posture, wiping off her tears with the back of her hand.

"I'm sorry. Yes, how can I help you?" she asked and my eyes widened at her response and her change in behaviour.

"Chahat—" I started.

"It's Ayushi, Mr Kapoor," she corrected me.

What the hell!

"Chahat, please," I said and a tear dropped from my eye.

Her eyes softened but they turned back hard again in no time.

"You left without an explanation and without a reason. You don't even have the slightest idea of what I have been through. No girl has entered my life. I became a workaholic; I became an alcoholic too! And here you are, living a good life! How?" I asked and cried in front of her.

There was a time when she would leave everything behind and take me in her arms if I cried.

"Mr Kapoor, I am sorry I can't do anything about that," she said.

"I need my answers," I said.

"I don't know what are you talking about," she said, looking away.

I didn't miss the tear that dropped on the other side of her face, justifying why she had turned her face away.

"I need my answers! I want to know why you left. I want to know why you disappeared. I want to know how your parents were reborn, but with different names! I want to know when your education turned private. I want to know how you were born in America. And most of all, how Chahat turned to Ayushi!" I said all at once.

She looked at me with shocked eyes.

"How do you know it all?" she asked.

"It doesn't matter. You tell me why," I repeated.

"No," she said, looking away again.

"Yes," I said.

"No," she said again.

"Yes," I shouted this time.

"No," she said, equally loud.

"Yes," I said without budging.

"What? What do you want to know? They are my parents! Don't you dare say anything about them. And why I left?" She started and looked at me with bloodshot eyes.

My heart broke at that sight.

"I left because I had my own reasons! I left because of the promise I made to myself, not to you! I left because I wanted the best for you. And I'll continue wanting the same, Aryan! It's better you forget me because I have already forgotten you. And Chahat? Chahat, doesn't exist. She is no more. She has died. The one standing here is Ayushi who loves her job, loves her parents and loves her best friend, Kajal," she said, crying, but her voice was strong. Strong enough to pierce right through my soul.

"*And I'll make sure Aryan and my children know every bit of their grandparents. Aryan and I will soon be a married couple. I am so blessed to have him. He's an amazing person.*"

I remembered her exact words which she had said in front of her parent's picture after their death.

"No," I said, my heart not able to accept the reality.

"Yes. And this is not Chahat speaking to her Aryan. This is Ayushi speaking to Mr Kapoor," Chahat said and her eyes were emotionless, just like her voice. I closed my eyes.

Reality hit me hard.

She made me realise that we were not what we used to be.

The crying in each other's arms was gone. Saying 'I love you' in every situation was gone. Holding each other tight was gone. Chahat and Aryan were gone.

What once was a nightmare, was now a reality.

Like Chahat, Aryan had also died and what was left was Ayushi and Mr Kapoor. Ayushi had a different story and life and I, too, had a different life now.

"*It is better you forget me, because I have already forgotten you!*"

Her words rang in my head again. It's time. It's time to move on.

"Mr Kapoor—" she started but I cut her off with my raised hand.

I opened my eyes that were completely red. She looked at me and her eyes softened, only to turn hard again.

I chuckled at the way her eyes had softened. She looked at me, shocked at the chuckle.

"Sorry for taking your time, Ms Chawla. Have a good day!" I said, and I hope she realised the difference between the time I used to call her 'Soon to be Mrs Kapoor' and today when I called her 'Ms Chawla'.

She was confused, but nodded nonetheless, and I turned my back to her. I moved forward and at the same time, I moved away from Chahat.

Five years ago, she had moved away and now, history was repeating itself. The only difference was that it was me this time.

Ms Ayushi Chawla, you are now history.

I wiped my tears, took a deep breath and walked out. Just when I turned to elevator, I saw it ding and Kajal came out.

"Aryan! What a surprise!" she said, surprised and smiled.

"Actually, I am done with the deal, so I'll be leaving tomorrow," I said.

"You don't look okay," she commented.

"I have a cold and I am a bit sick," I said.

"And then too you came to see me! I am so sorry that you had to wait. I was in a meeting. Did Ayushi meet you? Did she help you with some coffee or anything?" Kajal asked and I nodded.

"Ayushi!" Kajal called.

Chahat walked out and looked at Kajal and me.

"Did you take care of Aryan?" Kajal asked.

"She did," I said.

"That's good. Aryan, please take care of yourself," Kajal said as she held my hand. Chahat's eyes drew to our hands.

"I will," I said, smiling.

"Wait! Ayushi, just cancel the rest of my meetings for today. I am going with Aryan," Kajal said as she pulled me to her office.

She picked up her bag and we walked to the elevator. Chahat smiled at Kajal, but the smile didn't reach her eyes. It doesn't matter anymore, because I had taken my decision to marry Kajal.

∾

"We are going to miss you," Mr Pathania said as they came to see me off.

"Me too. Come to Mumbai soon," I said as we hugged. I met Kajal's mom too and then I went to Kajal.

"Be back soon! I had an amazing time!" she said and smiled at me.

"Definitely! You have to come to Mumbai now," I said and she nodded.

I landed in India and I was beyond tired. It was 12:30 a.m. and I directly went home and slept. The next day, I got ready later than my usual time and went down.

"Hello Aryan. How was America?" Mom said as she hugged me.

"Hi Mom. It was good. The deal is finalised, so it was worth it," I said.

"And you met Chahat too," Mom said.

"Yeah. It's good I met her or I wouldn't have moved on," I said, sitting down on the couch. Mom looked at me in shock.

"What?" I heard Siddhant and Abhi say.

I looked at the door and found those idiots there. I got up and hugged my brothers and we sat down.

"You moved on?" Abhi asked, unsure, to which I nodded.

"You must have got the answers to your questions. Tell us, why did she leave?" Siddhant asked.

"No, I didn't. I don't even need them. She doesn't love me," I said.

"She did," Mom pointed.

"Doesn't matter. I am ready to marry Kajal," I said.

"What?" they asked.

"Man, this guy has some serious issues. Kajal is Chahat's best friend," Abhi said.

"So?" I asked.

"I hope what you are doing is by your heart. I hope you are marrying Kajal because you want to and not because you want to hurt Chahat," Mom said.

I remembered the moment when Kajal and I walked out from Kajal's office. Chahat looked sad and upset when she saw Kajal holding my hand and that was the moment when I had decided that I was going to marry Kajal. That meant I was marrying Kajal because of Chahat, to make Chahat jealous and feel sad.

'No! It isn't that!'

"No," I said, more to myself than anybody else.

"That's good then. I am going to give your dad a call," Mom said and went away.

"Your expression says something else," Abhi said.

"What?" I asked.

"You still love Chahat," Siddhant said.

"If she doesn't, then why should I?" I asked and they both looked at each other.

"Look man, you've been through a lot. We have seen it all ourselves. We just want you to find true happiness," Abhi said.

"Exactly. We just want the best for you," Siddhant said.

I nodded and soon Mom came back. She told that dad had called Mr Pathania. After a few minutes, my phone buzzed.

Kajal: *Got the news. You made me really happy!*

I didn't know what to reply. I didn't know what I was thinking.

Aryan: *I'll try to make you happy.*

Kajal: *That's so sweet! I am lucky to have you.*

I shook my head. Why am I doing this to her when I don't love her?

You'll love her! She's beautiful, she's kind, she's always smiling and she's going to be a perfect wife!

Yes! I'll eventually love her! Not Chahat. I loved her, but that was the past. Kajal is going to be my future.

I replied with a smiling emoji before Siddhant and Abhi left.

Dad was very happy and said that the Pathanias were planning for the wedding very soon.

I nodded and talked to Kajal that night. I told her that I wanted to get married here in Mumbai. She respected my decision and we decided to get married here.

For her, it was just a normal request, but to me, it was a way to stay away from Chahat, because I knew she would make every possible excuse to not come to India. Even if she came, I would make sure to fill her up with the memories we had together and make her realise this was her real home.

Days passed. I talked to Kajal on a regular basis. We weren't that close yet, to talk about Chahat. She knew there was a girl in my life before her and she respected it. She had accepted that already and supported me with almost everything that went on in my life.

"Aryan," Dad said, while we were having dinner.

"Yes Dad?" I asked.

"The person we contacted for the date of the wedding said that next month is convenient for it. So, Mr Pathania and I are thinking that it would be perfect if Kajal and you get married by the end of next month," Dad said.

I thought for a while.

"You both know each other well too, so, it should not be a problem," Dad said, while Mom just concentrated on her food. Mom didn't talk to me much about the wedding after I returned from America.

'Probably because she knows that Chahat is still alive.' My inner voice said.

Chahat. She was supposed to be my wife! I wanted her to be my wife. I wanted her to be the mother of my children. I wanted her to be there with me everyday and every night. I wanted to grow old with her and live a happily ever after.

'But she doesn't love you!' My inner voice pointed out.

My hands tightened at that voice and the thought of her not loving me made me answer.

"I am fine with that. I am ready to get married in a month," I said.

∾

"I'll be coming to India in a week," Kajal said on the other side of the call.

"That'll be two weeks before the wedding functions," I said.

"Yes. Mom and Ayushi will be coming with me," she said.

My heart skipped a beat. Why?

"Great. I have a meeting. Can I call you later?" I asked.

"Yes, yes. Bye," she said.

We hung up and I just closed my eyes. I leaned my head back on my seat before there was a knock on my door and Dad walked in.

"Hey Dad," I said.

"Hi. You never told me you saw Chahat and found out some new and unexpected things," he said.

"Yes, Dad but it doesn't matter anymore. She doesn't love me," I said and chuckled bitterly.

"But she did," he said.

"Past is in the past. I am ready for my future," I said.

"But—" He started but I cut him off.

"Dad, please. Anyway, what brings you here?" I asked, changing the topic. Chahat's topic was too sensitive for me.

"Yes. I am here to tell you that we have finalised all the arrangements for the wedding – the place, the catering and all. You have to now finish off work quickly and go get your dresses for the functions. Also, you have to get a wedding ring for Kajal," he said.

I nodded and couldn't help but remember the proposal I had planned for Chahat. It took me months to find the perfect ring, weeks to plan the best proposal and days to prepare how I was going to get down on one knee, and to prepare the speech. Although it was different story that I forgot the speech and spoke whatever came to my mind, but I remember how Chahat cried and said yes and wore the ring. That night, we truly belonged to each other. I made love to her in a very intense way and promised that I was going to always take care of her, but destiny didn't want that. Despite my having proposed to her, she left.

"Aryan?" Dad called.

"Yes?" I asked.

"Where were you lost? I told you to ask Kajal whether you will both buy it together or individually," he said.

"Okay Dad. I will," I said and got up.

"I have a meeting now. I'll see you soon," I said as I buttoned my suit jacket.

Dad nodded and I got out of my office for the meeting which went on for two hours. I came back a bit exhausted. I looked at the time it would be in America and when it was convenient, I called Kajal.

"Hello?" she said.

"Hey," I said, sitting on my seat.

"Hi. How was the meeting?" she asked.

"It was good," I said.

"Great. Just a second," she said.

I replied with an okay.

"Ayushi, you just can't do this at the last moment. You had promised you will be going with me, along with Deepika aunty. I am not taking no for an answer. Book the tickets!" she said, on the other side.

I knew Chahat was going to do this, but now that she was coming, I was going to let all the memories come back to her and make sure she remembers every bit of it.

"Hey! What happened?" I asked when she picked up the phone again.

"Ayushi wasn't agreeing to come. I finally convinced her. Ayushi's mom is also coming," she said.

"Great. Listen, I guess it will be good if we buy the ring together," I said.

"Ring? Oh right! Yes, it will be great," she said.

"Great. So, I am leaving for home. You carry on with work," I said.

"Sadly, I have to, but anyhow, bye," she said, chuckling.

We hung up and I went home. The next one week went by in wedding preparations. Soon, the day arrived when everyone was coming to India from America. I went to the airport and met them all.

"Hey!" I said as I hugged Kajal, which caught her off guard. Chahat turned her gaze away from us.

"Hey," she said and pulled away. I met Kajal's mom and Chahat's so-called mom. It was the first time I saw her and I knew it was someone else.

"Hey Ayushi," I said. She tried smiling at me.

"Are you in Mumbai for the first time?" I asked, trying to get a reaction from her.

"No, no! She has been here before," her so-called mother came to her rescue.

I nodded and we all went towards my car. I had intentionally brought the car in which Chahat and I used to go on night drives.

Chahat kept looking at the car for a few minutes with sad eyes. I knew she was remembering all the times when she used to sit in the car on the passenger seat and we used to listen to the radio, sing songs, have our favourite food and even kiss. When she came out of her daze, she moved towards the passenger seat before reality hit her hard, when Kajal went ahead and sat on the passenger seat. Chahat slowly shut her eyes, took a deep breath and sat on the back seat.

'She has made herself strong over all these years.' My inner voice said as I started the engine.

"Mumbai is an amazing city," Kajal's mom said. "You're such a lucky girl, Kajal that you are going to spend your life with this amazing man in an amazing city," Kajal's mom added.

"That I am," Kajal said while I continued driving.

"Welcome, everyone," I said as we reached my home. They took in the beauty of the exterior of my home, except for one, who had been there a million times and every space here knew her by heart. Anyhow, Chahat's eyes were still taking in all the details of the place once again, remembering all the moments she had spent here.

Our maid, Mary, opened the door and when she saw Chahat, she started crying and hugged her. Mary had been here from the time I was born and she knew Chahat very well. Chahat was always sweet to her and found a motherly figure in Mary, just like I did. Mary always blessed us to be together forever and have many kids. Mary loved her and had cried a lot when Chahat had left.

"You're finally here! With my Aryan! I was happy when ma'am said that Aryan is coming with his future wife," she said and hugged her. Chahat couldn't control herself and hugged Mary, hiding her face in her shoulder.

Kajal and both aunties stood there confused.

"Mary, she's not Kajal," I said and it made Mary pull away from Chahat.

Mary looked at me with confused eyes as to why I had said that.

"She is my soon to be wife," I said as I pointed to Kajal and Kajal smiled at her.

Mary looked at me with shocked eyes. Her eyes went to Chahat and then to me and then to Kajal.

"She actually thought that Ayushi was going to be my wife," I said and they all nodded, understandingly.

"Hello everyone," Mom came out too, and finally, we all entered the house after the little scene.

Mom met everyone and stopped when she turned to Chahat. Mom kept looking at her and I knew she had started to tear up, but stopped and hugged her like she had hugged everyone else. Mom was extremely close to Chahat. She not only saw her as her daughter-in-law, but she loved her like her own daughter. Chahat had everyone's love and admiration, but it wasn't enough for her, I guess.

That day, we all had hours of conversation with Chahat, without speaking a single word.

"Ayushi, are you okay?" Chahat's so-called mom asked.

"Yes. I'll just go to the washroom," Chahat said and got up.

She turned the other way to go to the washroom when mom spoke suddenly, "Aryan, she doesn't know where the washroom is. Go and show it to her," Mom said and I realised that according to everyone else, she was coming here for the first time.

I nodded and stood up and we moved to the first floor. I knew there was a washroom downstairs too, but I don't know why I wanted her to come to my room. I opened the door to my room and she walked and used the washroom. Meanwhile, I sat on my bed.

"There was a washroom downstairs too," she said, making me look up.

"That has been placed for the maids," I said.

'Lie.' My inner voice said.

She nodded and her eyes went to her picture that was placed in my room. I followed her gaze and we both looked at our picture in which we both were smiling widely in Jodhpur, after we had fought over the girl who kissed me and created a misunderstanding between us.

"That day you had promised to love me forever and never leave my side. I wish people kept their promises," I said and chuckled bitterly.

"The same day when I promised myself that I am going to keep your life pure. I did keep my promise," she said and I raised my eyebrows.

Was she giving me a hint of why she left? Pure? Did she make my life pure by going away?

I looked at her hand and didn't find my ring which I had put on her. Her eyes followed my eyes and she lifted her left hand. She knew what I was looking at and she put her hand back and started to move back to the living area.

I followed her and we joined everyone. Soon, Dad joined us and we all had dinner together. Dad didn't react much and I was happy about that. He just nodded at Chahat and Chahat looked down. After dinner, they went to the guest rooms as Dad wasn't going to let anyone stay in a hotel.

That night, I hid our picture, as Kajal could come there anytime.

The next day, Kajal and I had to go to buy the engagement ring.

"We'll go in an hour," I said to Kajal on the breakfast table.

"Okay. Ayushi, you join us too," Kajal said.

"No, no. You both go," Chahat said.

"Oh, come on! You can get this chain replaced, maybe? For how long are you going to wear this locket? You have never even shown me its pendant. It's time for a change now!" Kajal said and I looked at Chahat's neck. I could see a chain, but her top hid the pendant.

"Oh yes! She got it for herself. She never even showed it to me. It sometimes interests me as to what she is wearing," Deepika aunty said.

"It's nothing. I really love this pendant, so I am not changing it. You both go ahead," Chahat said.

"Even if not for the chain, you're still coming. I need help with the ring and it was my dream to have my best friend with me throughout my wedding and its preparations," Kajal said.

"Please," Kajal's mother also said.

Chahat sighed but nodded. Soon, we left for the jewellery store.

"Hello. How can I help you?" the person asked, when we entered.

"We are here to buy engagement rings," I said.

He brought many boxes and kept them in front of us.

"Kajal, please see which one you like," I said.

"I'm not so good with these things. You decide for me," Kajal said.

"I can't decide. It once took me months to look for one," I said and stopped when I realised that I was going to give away too much information.

"Oh? It must have been a beautiful ring," Kajal said, knowing I was referring to my past.

"It wasn't good enough, I guess," I said.

"You guess?" she asked.

"If it were, then the person wouldn't be ashamed of wearing it," I said and I knew Chahat heard it.

"Oh!" Kajal said.

"Kajal, look at this. This is beautiful," Chahat said and picked one.

"I love it. Aryan, look!" Kajal said and showed it to me. It was pretty, but it was nowhere close to the one I had gotten for Chahat.

"It's good, but I feel we can get a better one," I said and asked the person to show some more.

The entire day, we looked for the ring and finally got one which we found the best. I observed Chahat throughout and I knew her eyes too well to know she was hiding a secret from all of us. Could I ask her what that secret was?

'But why should you? She doesn't love you! She isn't even wearing your ring! She would have worn it if it meant anything to her. She would have explained to you why she left if she loved you. She would have confessed her love for you. But she didn't. Let her go! Be with Kajal, marry her happily and stay away from Chahat!' My inner voice said.

I spent the next week mostly in my office. I hardly saw Chahat, or even Kajal. Kajal was busy with her dress fittings and all the other arrangements.

Just then, my phone rang.

"Hello?" I said.

"Aryan?" It was Dad.

"Yes Dad?" I asked.

"Pathanias are coming tomorrow. You have to be there to receive them, alright?" Dad asked.

"Right. I'll be there." I said.

"Good. Do you want to join us for coffee?" he said and I declined the offer before we hung up. I worked for an hour more before I left for home. I entered home and saw no one.

"Where is everyone?" I asked Mary while she served me dinner.

"They have gone out for a cup of coffee," she replied.

"Yes, I know, but why haven't they returned yet?" I asked.

"They will return soon," she replied.

I nodded and finished my dinner. After returning to my room, I slept and woke up to a knock at the door. I saw the time; it was 1:00 a.m. I yawned but got up to find Kajal outside.

"Hey," Kajal said.

"Hi," I said.

"Can I come in?" she asked.

"Oh yes! Please," I said.

We walked in and she sat on the bed.

"I know it's weird for me to come here like this and at this time, but I feel that we aren't close. We are about to get married and it still feels like we are not even good friends," she said.

"I am sorry I made you feel like that," I said, honestly.

"Yes, because it's a totally different feeling if we get to marry someone who we know like the back of our hands," she said.

I know Chahat like that.

'No, you don't. You would know her past too if you did.' My inner voice said.

"So, tell me about her," she said, smiling.

"Who?" I asked.

"The one who left you and made you like this," she said.

"Well, she was someone who was always smiling and once a person got to know her, they couldn't stop loving her. Well, that's totally like you. She was like you. Always smiling, always happy, always supportive," I said.

"That's so nice, but I am sure I am nowhere near her," she said.

"It's not like that. Everyone is different and you are the most beautiful girl in your own way," I said. "By the way, what about you?" I asked.

"About me?" She asked.

"Yes. You must not have been single all your life," I said, smiling.

"Well, I've had some relationships, but when I knew we weren't getting anywhere or they weren't someone I could love, I called it off," she said.

"Oh," I said.

She shrugged and we continued talking for hours. While I talked to her, I felt I was talking to a long lost friend. It felt good to talk to someone like that after so long.

"It was amazing! I finally feel my soon-to-be-husband is an amazing guy," she said.

"Hey! It isn't like you found me boring and not-so-good before," I said.

"Oh, believe me, you don't know the thoughts I have had about you," she said.

"Sorry to break this to you, but it sounded vulgar when you said it," I said, nonchalantly.

"Sorry to break this to you but 'vulgar' sounded disgusting when you said it," she said in the same tone.

"Whatever. Go to sleep," I said.

"Going to sleep, tall guy," she said and got up.

My heart started to beat faster at that nick-name. It was the name by which Chahat used to call me. I walked her to the door and shut it after she went to her room.

The next day, I went to the airport to receive Kajal's dad.

"Hello uncle," I said, as I met him.

"Start calling me Dad, son!" he said, hugging me.

"That's Naresh. Our family friend and Ayushi's father," Kajal's Dad introduced.

'He is not her father!' I thought.

"Hello," I said and he replied with a hello. We all left for home. After reaching, everyone talked while I just sat there.

"Aryan!" I heard, someone calling me from behind.

I turned around to see Kajal calling me.

"Yes?" I said.

"I have got your favourite! Waffles!" Kajal said as she raised the box.

"If I knew you would be nice enough to bring me some, then I would have told you this the first time we met," I said, joking.

"Your mistake. Come!" she said and we went to her room. She served me the waffles and I loved the taste of it.

"You were working?" I asked, eyeing her open laptop.

"Not really. Just going through some pictures," she said.

"Can I see?" I asked.

"Yes, yes, of course," she said.

I picked up the laptop and the first picture came on in which a young Kajal was smiling at the camera.

"You were funny," I commented.

"Cute would have done," she said, smiling, as she sat on the bed beside me and switched on the TV.

I clicked next and, in that picture, Kajal was having noodles and her lips was covered with sauce.

I laughed and I clicked on the next picture where Kajal was standing beside a beautiful girl. The girl looked like a model who had just walked a ramp. The background was that of a fashion show too.

"Who is she?" I asked, as I turned the laptop towards Kajal.

"Ayushi," she said, giving it a small glimpse.

Ayushi? Ayushi means Chahat, but this girl isn't Chahat! But she said Ayushi?

"Ayushi?" I asked, confused.

Kajal's eyes turned a bit wide at what she had said.

"I mean Ayushi's friend. Not Ayushi! Why would she be Ayushi?" Kajal said and laughed slightly.

"Anyway, leave it. Let's watch this movie. It is really great," Kajal said and took the laptop and kept it on the other side.

I knew something was suspicious there.

I turned to the movie, but my mind was on the picture. It was Ayushi, but it wasn't Chahat. Who was this? I thought Chahat only changed her name, but I was wrong. There was something more to this.

'I'll ask Chahat.' I thought.

'No! She won't tell you! It's clear! She took a different identity and she even stayed away for five years and so there's no chance that she'll tell you the secret easily.' My inner voice knocked some sense into me.

I can ask Kajal, but it won't be the best idea. So, now I have to find out what happened on my own.

The next day, I called Siddhant and Abhi from my office and told them everything about the picture.

"Maybe we can look for that girl," Siddhant said.

"Yes! It will be great and we can know what happened! Kajal's reaction made it clear that there's some link between this Ayushi and Chahat!" Abhi said.

"You're right Abhi! I'll just try my best to get her picture," I said.

We all agreed on it and I returned home. The next day, I got up slightly late as the previous night I was busy thinking how I could get her picture.

"Aryan?" Kajal's dad said while I was having my breakfast.

"Yes uncle?" I asked. I looked up and saw Kajal's dad with Chahat's so-called dad.

"Can you come with us to the wedding hall? We wanted to check it once, in person," he asked.

I agreed and we left for the hall. They were happy to find the hall more beautiful than they had imagined it to be.

"It was beautiful," Kajal's Dad said, on the way back.

"Yes, it was," Naresh uncle said.

"I am happy and sad at the same time. My daughter is getting married in just a few days," Kajal's dad said.

"Well, I also want Ayushi to agree to get married now," Naresh uncle said.

'Which Ayushi is he talking about?'

"Why? Is she not agreeing?" Kajal's dad said.

"Not at all. Well, after that day, you know," Naresh uncle said.

'Which day?'

"It has been five years now! I am going to talk to her," Kajal's dad said.

"What happened?" I asked.

"Just an incident. Oh look, we are here!" Kajal's dad said.

They got out of the car and I left for my office. My mind wouldn't stop thinking about what they were talking about. I came back early from work, directly went to Kajal's room and knocked on the door.

"Hey," she said after she opened the door.

"Hey," I said and I went in.

"What's up?" she asked.

"Nothing. I had sent an email to you. Did you check?" I asked while coming in.

"Oh! Sorry, I didn't. I'll check now," she said and opened her laptop. I sat there as she checked her mail.

"Hey guys!" Kaira and Samaira said as they entered the room, as planned.

"Hey Kaira and Samaira! Kajal, this is Samaira, Siddhant's wife and this is Kaira, Abhi's wife," I introduced them.

"Oh right!" Kajal said, smiling and got up immediately and went to meet them.

Kajal had her back to me as Kaira and Samaira kept her occupied.

"Kajal, come, we have got something for you. It's in the lobby," Kaira said and they took Kajal along.

I immediately took the laptop, opened her gallery but I didn't find the photo I had been looking for.

"Damn it!" I said. She must have deleted it.

I was about to close it, but I decided to check the recycle bin. I opened the recycle bin and looked for it. It was right there! She had deleted it. I took my phone out from my pocket and took its photo. I closed the recycle bin. I got up and moved down when I saw Kajal coming.

"They are really sweet! They got me this dress and we'll be going out for dinner tonight," Kajal said, excitedly.

"Great! So, you're changing?" I asked.

"Yes," she said.

"Okay. So, you change and have fun with the girls. I'm gonna be in my room," I said and she nodded.

I went to my room and messaged both my sisters saying thanks and mailed the picture to Siddhant and Abhi.

"She seems like a model to me. The background too seems like that of a fashion show," Abhi said.

"Exactly," Siddhant said.

"How do we find her?" I wondered before I spoke again.

"Guys! If we, by any way, know which fashion show it was, then we can easily find out about her," I said.

"Yes! My aunt's daughter is a model. I'll ask her if she knows which fashion show this is. I'll give her a call right away," Abhi said.

"Thanks, Abhi," I said, gratefully.

We hung up and I searched online, but couldn't find a clue. After an hour, Abhi called me again.

"Could you find something?" I asked.

"She said she can't say anything from just a picture. There are hundreds of fashion shows and she can't say anything just by the background," Abhi said.

"That's okay," I said before we hung up.

I didn't lose hope and started to look at the picture again to find even the slightest clue. I didn't find any so I decided to increase the brightness of my mobile as the background was black and I zoomed in. I looked patiently when I was able to see 'week' written on the background and a brand logo on the top.

That's it!

I decided to search about the brand and call them. I found the number on Google and called them right away.

"Hello? How may I help you?" The girl on the other side asked.

"Hello, I am Aryan Kapoor, the industrialist from Kapoor group of industries," I said.

"Oh yes! How can I help you, Mr Kapoor?" she said actively once she realised who I was.

"I need to get in touch with your manager," I said.

"Right away, Mr Kapoor," she said and I was connected to the manager.

"Hello, Mr Kapoor. How can we help you?" The manager asked.

"Hello. Actually, I wanted to know about a fashion week you had maybe sponsored in the past," I said.

"Sure. Which fashion week?" he asked.

"I am not sure about that," I said.

"Okay. How many years back then?" he asked.

"I don't have a good idea about that either," I said.

"I'm sorry sir, but we sponsor two fashion weeks every year and it would be difficult to tell which one you're asking about. Any hint you can give?" He asked.

"I have a picture of it and I am sure the fashion week I am talking about is before the last five years," I said.

I had a feeling by the way Kajal looked in the image, it was definitely not during the past five years.

"That'll make things easier. You just mail it to me and I'll check and get back to you," he said and I thanked him.

After we hung up, I sent him the image immediately.

The next day, Chahat, Kajal and everyone else left for the resort as they would be staying there for the rest of the days until our wedding. After they left, my relatives reached. They all were very excited about my wedding.

"Finally, it looks like there is a wedding in this house," Mom said, laughing.

"Yes, it does look like it. I am so excited to meet the girl who finally got our Aryan to marry her," my aunt said.

"Yes! I really want to meet her," my other aunt said.

"You all will meet her day after tomorrow during the *mehendi* and *haldi* ceremony," Mom said.

"Oh, I can't wait! Then the next day is the engagement?" one of them asked.

"Yes, and then the wedding," Mom said.

Around 11, when I was about to sleep, I got a call from the manager of the brand.

"Hello?" he said on the other side.

"Hello. Were you able to find something?" I asked.

"I am sorry for calling so late. I had to seek permission from our CEO. Also, it took me almost the entire day but I was able to find it. This picture is of the fashion week we sponsored six years back. The background in the picture helped me identify the fashion week as every fashion week we sponsor has a different theme," he said.

"Oh! Thank you so much. Can I get the name of the model?" I asked.

"I'm sorry but we don't have the name," he said.

"That's okay. Thanks for the information." I said.

"You're welcome. It's great we could be of help to you," he said and we were about to hang up when a question struck my mind.

"Wait! How do you get the models?" I asked.

"We only sponsor the fashion week, and have no idea about that as it's the designers who get the models for their clothes," he said.

"So, can you please ask the designer?" I asked.

"Sure. I'll call the designer and tell you how they get models maybe by day after, as tomorrow is an off. Will that be okay?" He asked.

"Absolutely! Thank you so much for the help!" I said.

"You're welcome, Mr Kapoor. I wish this improves the relations between our companies as well," he said.

"Definitely," I said.

"It's a pleasure to have good relations with your company, sir. Thank you and good night," he said and we hung up.

'Soon, Chahat. Soon I'll know why you left me,' I thought before sleeping. The next day passed with the preparations for the function and soon it was the day of the *mehendi* ceremony.

"Aryan, are you ready?" Siddhant asked.

"Yes," I said.

"So finally, Aryan is all ready to get married," Abhi said and I nodded.

"Let's go," I said.

We all left for the resort where the ceremonies were to be held. The ceremonies were organised beside the pool. After some time, I saw Kajal walking in with Chahat. Kajal looked beautiful in her yellow dress, but Chahat... she looked gorgeous and stunning. The only thing missing on her face was a smile, while Kajal had a glow on her face. Kajal came and stood beside me. She smiled at me and I smiled back at her.

"Come, both of you! We'll start with the *haldi* ceremony," Mom said.

Kajal and I nodded and we sat down on the couch for the ceremonies. There was music, food, dance and happiness all around, but all these things didn't matter. My eyes only looked for Chahat, but she wasn't around. I didn't see her after she came along with Kajal.

"Look, how beautiful they look together!" Kajal's mom said.

"They are made for each other, aren't they?" Kajal's dad said.

"She is gorgeous!" my aunt said.

Kajal sat down to have henna applied on her hands while I got up after a while. I saw a missed call from the manager.

"Hello?" I said.

"Mr Kapoor, I talked to the designer and she said that they have a contract with an academy that trains models," he said.

"Okay. What is the name of the academy with which she has a contract?" I asked.

"Wings Modelling Academy," he said.

"I got that! Thanks once again," I said.

"Anytime," he said and disconnected the call.

I went inside and called the modelling academy to get details of Ayushi.

"Hello? How can the Wings Modelling Academy help you?" the girl on the other side said.

"Hello, I am Aryan Kapoor, from the Kapoor group of companies," I said.

"Oh yes! How can we help you, sir?" she asked in a sweeter voice. Sometimes I thanked my stars for my name, and more so now, as it could get me some information easily.

"I wanted to seek information about one of your models," I said.

"Okay sir. I'll connect you with Mr Ajay, who can help you with that," she said before I was connected to Mr Ajay.

"Hello, Mr Kapoor," he said.

"Hello, Mr Ajay. I wanted to get some information about a model," I said.

"Yes, I was informed. So, please tell me the name and I'll give you any amount of information we can offer," he said.

"I'm not sure about her name, but she participated in a fashion week, about six years back that was sponsored by a fashion brand. Also, I have a picture of her and I'll mail it to you," I said.

"Sir, it's difficult to know who you are talking about with this little information, but send me the picture and it might be of some help," he said.

"Sure. I'll just send it and you can get back to me," I said.

We hung up and I sent him the picture.

I went back outside and saw Kajal laughing and getting her henna done. I sat beside her. It was already evening and Chahat was still not here.

"Where is your friend?" I asked Kajal.

"Ayushi? She's having a back ache. She's resting," she said.

'Again, Chahat is lying.' My inner voice said.

I just know her too well! She didn't want to attend this function. We sat there for some more time while everyone danced, got drunk, had food and all the lights turned on as it was already dark. Everyone was clearly having a lot of fun as no one was ready to leave the dance floor. After it was late at night, everyone started leaving.

"Meet you tomorrow, Aryan," Kajal said.

"Sure. Bye," I said as Kajal hugged me and smiled at me before she went to her room with her cousin.

"She's nice," Dad said, behind me.

"She is," I said.

"So, finally you're over Chahat?" Dad said as he stood beside me.

I didn't reply as I kept looking out in space.

"You know, Aryan, since you were a kid, you have always been a jolly kid. You always laughed, joked and lived in the moment. You grew up and your smile only grew with time. You met Siddhant and Abhi, who were not less than your brothers. Then, Chahat came into your life. I only saw you smiling and being genuinely happy. You loved her like she was a part of you. After she left, I lost my son. I lost the smile on my son's face," Dad said.

I listened quietly.

"Now, he's getting married and she's also here. The funny part is that it's not only my son, but also her, who has lost her smile. I am your father, Aryan, but I considered her my daughter too. She has lost her parents and brother. I don't know what happened that made her leave and I don't know what is destined to happen, but I only want the best for you both. Aryan, find your happiness. Give me my Aryan, my old son back. If it's with Kajal, go to her, and marry her, but please give my son back to me. Maybe seeing you happy, Chahat will decide to smile again," Dad said, patted my back and left.

The next day, I was in deep thought when mom came.

"Aryan?" Mom's voice came.

"Yes?" I asked as I came out of my daze.

"Here are your clothes. Please get ready in an hour. We have to leave for the engagement," she said as she kept my clothes on my bed and turned around.

After she left, I got a call.

"Hello?" I said.

"Hello, Mr Kapoor? This is Ajay from Wings Modelling Academy," he said.

"Oh yes, Ajay. Could you find who she is?" I asked.

"Yes, I was able to find it," he said and started telling me about her and the more I got to know about her, the more shocked I was.

Ayushi Chawla.

I got ready in my black suit and I was still reeling in the information. Siddhant and Abhi were there with their families. I told them all that I had got to know about Ayushi and they were beyond shocked. The only thing that was bothering us now was how Chahat was related to Ayushi.

We all left for the resort. We entered the engagement hall and I went to the stage for the ceremony. Kajal walked in with Chahat at her side. Chahat was looking beyond gorgeous in her golden dress. Kajal looked beautiful too, with a beautiful smile on her face, and in a blue and golden dress. A bride with an amazing glow! Kajal stood next to me and Kajal's cousin came with a tray that had the same two rings we had bought. Kajal put the ring on my finger and I looked at Chahat but Chahat had her back to me and she moved away. The fireworks went off and rose petals fell on us. Everyone including Kajal looked at the fireworks, but I looked at Chahat. Chahat, kept moving away, without looking back and I saw her open the balcony door and leave the hall. Kajal looked at me, with confused eyes and pointed at the ring. I diverted my gaze and without thinking, put the ring on her ring finger because suddenly I wanted to get done with it as soon as possible. I suddenly wanted to go after Chahat.

The moment I put the ring in her finger, music started playing and everyone gathered around us, blessing and congratulating us. More than an hour passed by and still there were guests who were coming and getting pictures clicked with us and congratulating us. When we were finally left alone, I got off the stage and went around when I saw Chahat talking to a guy and drinking. Immediately, I saw nothing but red. How dare he!

"Aryan," Kajal said, behind me.

"Yes?" I asked.

"What are you doing here?" she asked.

"I came here to get a drink," I lied.

"Oh! Take it from a waiter. Let them have their time," Kajal said.

"They?" I asked, pointing at Chahat and that guy.

"Yes. This guy has been after Ayushi for so long now, but she doesn't even look at him. I am glad they are having their own time," she said.

My blood boiled and my relaxed hands turned into fists. I looked at Chahat when she was having shots. She didn't drink before. What happened now? And she was drinking with some guy, who was clearly into her! What about her safety?

"Come," Kajal said and held my hand and pulled me along with her.

Kajal stopped beside her mother and Chahat's so-called mother. I looked around to spot our group. I saw Samaira and Kaira talking to Diya. I knew I couldn't go there, so I immediately went to a safe distance and called Samaira.

"Hi Aryan. What's up?" she asked.

"Hi. Actually, Chahat is drinking and I want Kaira, Diya and you to keep an eye on her," I said.

"Drinking? Chahat? She never drank!" she said, worried.

"That was in the past," I said.

"Don't worry. We'll keep a check on her," she said and I thanked her before I moved towards Kajal who was still talking to her and Chahat's mom.

"I am happy about them. Ayushi needs to move on," Kajal's mother said.

They didn't know I could hear them.

"I was worried about Ayushi. After what happened five years back, she has been punishing herself," Chahat's so-called mom said.

"She's one strong girl! It's not easy, what she did. It's not easy to give up everything," Kajal's mother said.

"Yes, I know. But she gave up everything because she feels she became the person she hated the most," Chahat's so called mom said.

"The same day when I promised myself that I am going to keep your life pure. I did keep my promise."

"I had my own reason to leave."

I remembered Chahat's words.

"That's Ayushi."

Kajal called a model Ayushi and then deleted her image after I saw it. It's obvious they were hiding some big secret.

The thing was I knew all about Ayushi, but how she was related to Chahat was still a mystery. I knew Chahat never knew someone called Ayushi and there wasn't even any means by which they would know each other, so how the hell did Chahat become a part of this!

"She became the person she hated the most."

"After what happened five years back, she has been punishing herself."

What exactly happened five years back? What made Chahat a part of it all? What happened that Chahat is punishing herself? What happened that she became the person she hated?

The entire episode was stressing me out and I wanted to get some fresh air. I went to the balcony that was quite away from the engagement hall. I moved out and closed my eyes as the wind blew, calming my mind and heart. It was good that the place was away from the hall as no one would come there to disturb me and take me back in.

"It's now I realise that I am nothing without you. My life has no meaning without you. Aryan Kapoor, I love you and I promise that I am never going away. I'll always be with you. Always."

My old Chahat's words came to haunt my mind.

We had hugged tightly after that and we had been inseparable.

It was the time when we believed that our souls and hearts were meant to be each other's. We were in love with each other with everything we had. It was when she was about to take my surname in a few days. It was when she was about to be the mother of our children. But before anything could happen, she left me.

A tear dropped from my eye.

Chahat, you left despite promising me you won't.

Why had our destiny been so cruel to us? Why?

My phone rang bringing me back.

"Hello?" I said, but the signal was weak.

"Damn," I muttered and moved to a side that was a bit dark to get the signal.

"Hello?" I said again.

"Hello? Rahul?" the person said.

"No, it's Aryan Kapoor," I said.

"Oh, sorry. My mistake," the person said.

"No worries," I said and we hung up.

I started to take a step to move back to the hall, but I stopped in my track as I saw the door of the balcony open and Chahat walked out of the door and closed it behind her. She stood where I had been standing a few minutes back. I kept looking at her from the dark side of the balcony.

She looked at the moon or maybe the stars.

"Hey mom. Hey dad. How are you both?" she said and her eyes sparkled.

"As every other night, I am back in front of you and talking to you. So finally, Kajal is engaged. She is such a nice girl and she deserves happiness, unlike me. Isn't it?" she said.

"Chahat Aggarwal. It feels so good to take that name again. This name is now faded. It's dead. You know what, if you two were alive today, then nothing would have gone wrong. I would now have been Chahat Aryan Kapoor, happily married to the one I have loved all my life. But I can't blame anyone, because a person like me took your lives," she said, smiling bitterly.

A person like her? What does that mean?

"You know it breaks me every time I tell Aryan that I have forgotten him when the reality is there hasn't been a single day when I have not remembered him and us. What a beautiful time we had spent. How close we were! How beautiful my life was!" she said, chuckling.

"But now it's all burned and all that is left are the ashes. I am still living with those ashes. How I wish, that night had never happened! How I wish, I didn't hear my phone ringing! How I wish I woke Aryan up! How I wish my phone hadn't broken and the hospital people had gotten Aryan's number. I wish Naresh Dad and Deepika Mom had found his number and called him when I was in the bed, in blood and fighting for my life! How I wish that I hadn't made it and had died in the hospital, or maybe on the road itself and come to you both! Death would have been better than this pain, isn't it? We would have lived happily in heaven together. You both, Ayushi and I," she said, crying.

Hospital? Blood? Fighting for life?

But this is not the time for my answers!

How could she even think that! How could she think that it was better if she died! Doesn't she think about me? Doesn't she care what would have happened to me if she died?

A tear dropped from my eye.

Chahat had gone through so much in these past five years! But why? And how? How did she land in such a situation?

"But death isn't so easy. I stayed alive because if I died, the beautiful relation I shared with Aryan would have died too. I am living with the memories of it. I am alive for my Aryan. Mom, Dad, I have made mistakes in my life and I am paying for them all for the past five years, but it never hurt this much. It never hurt this much when I remembered our old times. Now, even standing here is breaking me. I am feeling a pain in my chest when I remember Kajal putting the ring on Aryan's finger. I dreaded seeing Aryan putting a ring on her finger so I came here to be with both of you. Only you both and I know how much I have missed my Aryan. It's breaking me. I am leaving tomorrow. I can't take it. I'll die like this! I miss him. I miss you. I miss my old life. How can god be so cruel to me!" Chahat said as she fell on her knees and cried hard. Tears ran down my cheeks as a sob left my mouth.

Chahat's eyes opened wide when she looked up and spotted me standing there with tears in my eyes. Chahat kept looking at me, wide-eyed with tears that were drying on her face. She slowly got up.

"Chahat Agarwal. You know who she is? The girl who made me believe in love. The girl who made me feel special. The girl who made me believe in the saying that 'there's a woman behind every successful man'. The girl who was always positive, sweet and kind, no matter what. The girl who was the reason behind my existence," I said as I moved towards her and she sobbed.

"When she left, my world collapsed. I kept looking at my phone again and again, thinking Chahat would call me. I kept waiting that she'll come and say 'Sorry Aryan, I got late'. I waited for five years. I put my mind in work. I became a workaholic and was even on the verge of becoming an alcoholic. I kept crying myself to sleep whenever I missed her. I forgot how being happy felt. I didn't know where she was or whether she was alive, but my love for her didn't fade, and look at destiny! It brought my Chahat back to me! But she said she hated me and has already forgotten me. She did everything she could by controlling her tears and being rude to me, so that I believed she has moved on. But no! Now I know how much she still loves me!" I said, tears dropping from my eye while she was also crying hard.

"Tell me, Chahat! Tell me what happened that night! Tell me whose call that was! Tell me how you landed in a hospital! Tell me who those two are, who you call your parents! Tell me all of it!" I demanded.

"No matter how much I wish things had happened any other way, I feel it's just karma that's after me for what I did," Chahat said.

"That's not the answer to my question," I said.

"Some questions are better left unanswered, Aryan. I agree I didn't want it all to happen, but that doesn't mean I even have the right to make it right. Some things aren't in our hands, it's in our fate. Also, you know how I always believed that everything happens for a reason. I still believe the same. So, you should know you didn't hear the call ringing for a reason. Naresh Dad and Deepika Mom didn't call you for a reason. I fought alone for my life for a reason. And today, we are beside each other but not together, for a reason. We are at your wedding, but I am not the bride, is also for a reason. And it's better that you and I accept it. You have to be with Kajal. You both deserve happiness, not me. I am just getting in between. And it is good that you heard me, so I wouldn't have any regrets, Aryan. It's time I should leave. Bye," she said and she turned to leave. She kept walking as I kept looking at her.

No! She can't leave me! She just can't leave me once again!

I have to stop her, but how!

Should I tell her everything I know? Maybe it could stop her!

"Ayushi Chawla, the popular model," I started and she stopped dead in her tracks.

Chahat slowly turned towards me.

"A famous model who was Naresh and Deepika Chawla's only daughter, born and raised in America, did a lot of fashion shows. She had a boyfriend in Mumbai and maybe that's why she came there to Mumbai and started to learn modelling, in Wings Modelling Academy. She walked on a ramp in a fashion week, six years ago in Mumbai. After a year, she was about to get married in Mumbai to her boyfriend. Sadly, a few days before her wedding, she lost her life in an accident and that was five years ago," I said confidently, remembering all the information Ajay had provided me with.

Chahat looked at me with shock, her mouth open wide.

"How? How do you know all this?" she asked.

"Just in an attempt to know why you left me," I said.

Chahat kept looking at me, still recovering from what I had said.

"Chahat, the identity you live with is not false, but it's someone else's. I know everything about Ayushi. I know everything about you, but the only thing I don't know is how you are related to Ayushi!" I said.

"Some mysteries aren't meant for everyone to know," Chahat said, with sparkling eyes as if she would cry any moment.

"Everyone? Am I everyone to you? Am I an outsider in your life, Chahat? I am the one who could turn mountains for you! I am the one who sent all his people in search of you when you left! I am the one who hated shopping, but happily spent months looking for your ring! And you call me an outsider? Sorry, Chahat Aggarwal, but I am not an outsider! I am the one whose ring you wore!" I said.

"But not now. I don't wear it now," she said, bitterly.

"Stop lying, Chahat! Stop acting as if you don't love me anymore! Stop playing with me! Do you think I am dumb? Do you think I don't know that it's not a pendent but my ring that you have put in that chain?" I said, remembering seeing how her pendant, which was my ring, came into view when she fell on her knees a few minutes back.

She closed her eyes.

"Chahat, please tell me. Please, tell me how you are related to Ayushi. Please, Chahat," I said but she shook her head in a 'no'.

She turned around and started to move away.

"Chahat please. Tell me!" I kept repeating it all the while.

When she kept moving away, and wasn't stopping, I went near her and held her wrist and turned her around to face me.

"Why can't you tell me? How are you related to Ayushi?" I asked, with my voice loud and Chahat's wrist still in my hand and tears falling from her eyes.

"How am I related to Ayushi? What do I tell you? How do I tell you that I am her murderer?" Chahat said, crying badly.

My world stopped and my face lost its colour.

No! She can't be. She's lying. She can't be.

"What?" I asked.

"Yes! I am the one who killed her," Chahat said, crying,

"I hated criminals! I hated people who kill other people. I hated people who caused road accidents and I became just that! First, my brother lost his life to some criminals, then, my best friend almost lost her life in a road accident, then, my parents died in a road accident and then me. I caused a road accident that took away Ayushi's life and I was on the verge of losing mine as well," Chahat said, crying hard.

It was all a lot to take in.

"Tell me everything that happened that night.," I demanded.

I sighed internally when she nodded. It was probably because she had lost all her energy to fight with me over it again.

Chahat

A day before the funeral

"Hello, Mr Deep Singh?" I asked.

"Speaking, who is it?" He asked.

"I'm Chahat. Your brother, Mr Singh, gave me your number. He owns a gallery that showcases my paintings," I said.

"Yes, yes. He told me that you paint some amazing work and you needed some help," he said.

"Thank you and yes, I need your help. Actually, my parents died in a car accident today afternoon," I said, a sob leaving my mouth.

"Oh, I am so sorry," he said.

"I have been informed it was a hit and a run case," I said.

"And me being an investigator, you want me to find the person?" he asked.

"Yes. Please," I said.

"You could have asked the police," he said.

"I was thinking I could, but I feel it's better if I get it done by a known person. You're Mr Singh's brother and like a brother to me too. I can trust you," I said.

"Don't worry, Chahat. I'll forward you a few questions about your parents and the accident and you have to answer them and send me. Will it be okay?" he asked.

"Absolutely. Thank you so much," I said.

"No worries and be strong," he said and we hung up. Soon, he sent me questions like what were their names and on which road did the accident take place and also asked me to attach the pictures of my parents. I planned on answering them after the funeral.

'I will tell Aryan once I have some information in my hand.' I thought.

The next day, I answered all the questions and sent them back to Mr Deep Singh.

After two weeks, it was Samaira's wedding day and I was getting ready for her wedding function while Aryan was in the washroom.

My phone buzzed.

Deep Singh: *I have some information related to the death of your parents.*

Chahat: *Alright. When can you tell me?*

Deep Singh: *I'll tell you all about it in person tomorrow?*

Chahat: *Sure, that's totally fine. Thank you so much.*

Aryan and I left for the wedding and we got back late. We were tired and slept directly.

My phone started ringing and that woke me up.

"Who could it be?" I wondered.

"Hello?" I said.

"Hello, Chahat. I am so sorry to disturb you," Deep said.

"Hello. No, it's alright. Tell me," I asked.

"Actually, my grandmother lived in Canada and she passed away just after I spoke to you and now, I have to leave for Canada immediately," he said.

"Oh, I am so sorry," I said.

"No, it's okay. I wanted to tell you that my brother and I won't be back for a long time as we have to be in Canada," he said.

"So, what about the information about my parents' death?" I asked.

"I tried calling you several times. I quickly got a visa through my contacts. It's already 4 a.m., and I have a flight at 9. So, will it be okay if you see me before I leave?" he asked.

"You mean now?" I asked.

"Yes. I already have the information about it, you just have to come, collect the file and I'll tell you a few things and then you are free to go. At least after that, I won't be leaving an unsatisfied client behind," he said.

I rubbed my forehead. If I said yes, I'd come back soon and also have the file with me and if I said no, I'd have to get another investigator who I wouldn't know and trust as much I trusted Deep.

"I'm coming. Just text me the address and I'll be there," I said.

"Thank you, Chahat. I am sorry for all this trouble, but I know this is important to you," Deep said.

I brushed and washed my face. I left a note for Aryan, just in case he got up before I reached home.

I looked at him, sleeping soundly.

He was really tired from yesterday night. After all, it was his best friend's wedding, he had to dance till his feet hurt. I moved near him and kissed his cheek once before I left the room.

I sat in my car and looked at that address. I started to drive towards it and turned on the radio. I stopped at the red light and witnessed the sun rising along. I looked around while driving and felt that by mistake I had taken a wrong turn. The beautiful sunrise and music had distracted me. I shook my head and continued to drive while I took my phone out and turned on the GPS.

I was setting the address in it while driving. I finished setting it and looked up on the road. All of a sudden, I spotted a girl jogging, with headphones, on the roadside. I tried my best to turn my car at the last moment, but it was too late and she got hit. In my attempt to save her, I also hit my car on a pole and my head banged on the steering wheel. The last thing I remembered was the windshield breaking and glass falling on me.

I felt a sharp pain in my head and my eyes closed to darkness.

∾

The next time I opened my eyes I was in a hospital room.

"Aryan?" I said, unknowingly.

"She's awake," the nurse said and a couple I had never seen before, came in with a doctor.

"How are you feeling?" The doctor asked.

"Severe pain in my head," I said as I tried getting up.

"No, no, dear. Rest," the woman said.

"Take the medicines and rest, as much as possible," the doctor said and left.

I looked at the couple.

"Are you fine, dear?" they asked.

"Yes," I said.

They looked at each other and sat down beside me.

"Hi. You must be thinking why we are here and who we are," the woman said and I nodded.

"I am Deepika Chawla and he's my husband, Naresh Chawla. We live in the US. We came to India as our daughter, Ayushi, was getting married here," she said with teary eyes.

Her husband kept an arm around her to support her and he, too, had teary eyes.

"She went out for a jog as she wanted to look radiant and fit during her wedding, but she didn't come back. We got worried and later we got the news that our daughter, Ayushi had died in a road accident," she said.

No! No! Please God, don't let it be what I feel it is. Please! Please!

"We came to get her body when we found out that it was your car that hit her. You tried to save her, and in an attempt to do that, you hit yourself too. You had head injuries so bad that if a passer-by had not moved you to the hospital immediately, you would have died due to loss of blood on the road itself. The hospital had your blood type and they were able to save you just in time," the man said.

My eyes got wide and my hand went on my mouth. My eyes turned watery.

I caused a death. A person who was about to get married in a few days, who was going to be a bride, light up the home of someone, had died because of me. This couple had lost their daughter because of me. They were crying because of me.

I am a monster! I am just like the person who killed my parents and my little brother.

Oh god! I am a murderer! I am a criminal! I am a monster!

Tears started falling from my eyes. What had I done!

"Hey! Hey! Calm down," the woman said.

"I killed your daughter! How can you be so nice to a person like me? How can you be so kind to a monster like me? I don't deserve it," I said, crying.

"We know you've lost your parents a few days back," the woman said.

"We came to see you here and didn't have the slightest idea of who you were, but one of the hospital persons knew your name as a friend of yours was admitted here a few months back and you used to visit her. Later when we tried to know about you, we discovered that your parents were no more and you didn't have any relative here," the man said.

"We were very angry and I hated you. Which mother won't hate the person who killed her daughter? But after we got to know about you, I realised you were going through the same pain, and imagining the pain you would have felt, melted me. I didn't hate you anymore. Maybe god had decided to take away one daughter and give me another," the woman said, making me cry more.

"Dear, we have lost one daughter, but god has decided to give us another one. God has taken your parents away, but see, he has given you us and we are never going to let you feel that you have lost your parents," the man said and my heart warmed.

"Me too. I am never going to let you both feel you have lost your daughter. I am going to love you like my own parents. Maybe, that's how I could fill this grief of yours," I promised, with tears.

The woman started crying and hugged me.

"You are my daughter, now. Just like my Ayushi," she said.

I nodded and hugged her back.

"When did the accident take place?" I asked.

"Fifteen days back. You have been out for two weeks," they said.

Aryan doesn't know where I have been for two weeks!!

"Now, get recovered dear and we all will go back to America," she said. "And yes, we found this," she said as she gave me a ring.

My eyes fell on the ring that Aryan had given me. I took it and kept looking at it.

How could I wear it on? How could I be Aryan's fiancé? How, when I was the one who took away someone's love? How, when I caused the death of the girl who was going to be a bride, just like I was going to be?

I have no right to marry and be a bride. I have no right to be someone's love when I took away someone's love.

I don't deserve happiness. I committed a crime for which I will have to repent all my life. From now on, I will only give happiness and not expect anything in return. From now on, I will only live for these two and for the memory of the beautiful relationship I shared with Aryan.

"I will go to America with you both," I said as I held the ring.

"Are you engaged? It looks like an engagement ring," she said.

"No. I had liked it so I bought it," I lied.

Aryan, I promised to make your life pure and I have to leave in order to keep your life pure. I know you would be hurt, but soon, you'll get yourself together and find a pure girl to marry and be happy with.

I am going to miss the guy with whom I planned a happily ever after. I am going to miss the couple who were going to be my in-laws, but already treated me like their own daughter, the girls, who were no less than my sisters, and the guys, who were not less than my brothers and protected me with everything they had.

I am going to miss my life.

Kajal

"Kajal, where is Aryan?" Mom asked me.

"I don't know. I'll check," I said.

"I'll come with you," she said.

"No, Mom. You be here and I'll get him," I said and looked around. I saw a door that led to a balcony.

'Maybe he's there,' I thought and opened the door. I had to walk a bit to reach the balcony. I saw Aryan but I also saw Ayushi there.

Aryan was holding her by the wrist.

What's happening here?

"Chahat, you have suffered so much. Why didn't you ever tell me or contact me?" Aryan said.

How does he know her name was Chahat?

"Aryan, I had taken the life of a bride and someone's love. I didn't deserve your love. I knew you would have suffered and missed me, but you deserved to have a pure life, untouched by any wrong," Chahat said, crying.

"Chahat, you can never be impure. I lost myself when you left. You don't know what my condition was, but now I know that your condition was worse than mine," Aryan said, crying.

"Aryan, I have always loved you. I used to look at your pictures online. I kept looking at your ring. I carried you wherever I went," Chahat said.

"You don't know how much I love you. You are everything I need. When I saw you again, I felt I had got my oxygen back," he said.

A tear fell from my eye.

So, she was the one who he always talked about. She was the one who left him.

I smiled bitterly at the reality.

Just when I thought he had started feeling something for me and when I had fallen completely in love with Aryan, I got to know that Aryan loved Chahat.

"But we can't get back together. I am happy that now you won't live with any questions about why I left you. I know Kajal is the best for you. She is an amazing girl and she'll keep you happy," Chahat said.

"Why? You love me and I love you and now we have cleared everything, then why?" Aryan asked.

"Aryan, I still am the same impure girl. I am still the one who killed Ayushi. I can't," Chahat said.

"No, you don't have to feel this way," Aryan said.

"Aryan, your saying this won't change anything. Please, I am not the one for you. You don't know how difficult it is for me, but I have to leave. Bye, Aryan Kapoor. I will always love you. Have an amazing life ahead," Chahat said, taking a deep breath.

I turned around and hid in the corner of the balcony.

"Chahat, please," Aryan said.

"Aryan, please. Kajal deserves you and loves you. Be happy. Get married to her and have amazing kids. I just wish the best for you both. Keep coming to America. I would love to see a little you or maybe a little Kajal. How beautiful they will look! They are going to be my favourite children! It would be such a nice feeling to play with them and to see you and Kajal be the best parents. Aryan, I always wished the best for you and you're getting it. Not every love lasts forever and we have that love. Keep smiling and I wish you a good and happy married life." Chahat said, crying and soon turned and left.

"Why? God, why do you always do this? Why us? Why Chahat and me? I have loved her with everything I had. I don't know many people who love like this, but the ones like us, who love like this, always suffer! First, she went away for five years and now she is going forever. It seems my only dream and my only wish will never become a reality," Aryan shouted and cried.

I turned around, left the balcony and went to my room. I texted my mom that I wasn't well and had to sleep. The moment I entered my room, I let loose my emotions. I cried with the burden of the words I had just heard.

I cried as I had lost the only guy I ever loved. I cried as the girl who was always my friend and supporter had suffered too much in her life. I cried as I never realised the pain behind every single time she smiled.

I cried because two people who were in love couldn't be together.

Is love like that?

Yesterday, I was so happy, getting married to the one I love. But today, reality hit me hard.

"*You're so tiny.*" Aryan's voice rang in my head, making me smile.

He always was like this, jolly. The only thing was that I thought behind his jolliness was a guy who felt something for me. But now I know, behind his jolliness was a guy who was in pain as he had lost his love.

I smiled.

Love is such a beautiful thing that one is willing to sacrifice one's own happiness, just so the other one can be happy.

Some things in life happen on their own, but some need effort. Often, we think that it isn't meant to be and give up, but we always fail to realise that everything is meant to happen if done the right way.

We have to put patience, love and effort, and without these things, we can't make anything happen.

These two had tried patience and love, but they forgot effort.

'Aryan and Chahat, maybe you have given up on your love and your ways have parted, but for the love I have for Aryan, I am going to help you both to put the effort and make you both finish your chase for your love,' I thought.

Aryan

"Aryan, are you ready?" Mom asked.

I nodded. Mom smiled and left.

"Aryan, are you sure?" Abhi asked.

I nodded.

"You've been quiet since morning," Siddhant said.

"I don't want to talk," I said.

"I don't think this is the reason," Siddhant said.

"It is the reason," I said, although I knew I was lying.

Chahat was the reason. Today, I was going to marry Kajal and I had no way left by which I could be with Chahat. It was too late and I had lost all hope.

I sighed and my phone buzzed.

I looked at it and saw a message.

Kajal: *Just couldn't sneak out with all these people around earlier. Can you meet me in the balcony?*

My eyebrows furrowed. Why does Kajal want to see me?

Aryan: *Sure. I'll see you in 5.*

I, after being interrogated by those two idiots, went to the balcony and saw Kajal there. She was facing towards the other side and turned when she heard my footsteps. She was all ready and wearing her bridal lehenga and jewellery, but her hair was undone.

"You look pretty," I said and she smiled at me.

"Thank you and you look very handsome," she said, her eyes trying to dig deeper into my eyes.

"Thank you. Is everything okay?" I asked.

"Aryan, you know, my friend, Ayushi? Her name isn't Ayushi. It's Chahat," she said.

My heart started to beat fast when I heard her name. Why is she talking about it?

"Chahat came into my life five years back and we have been friends ever since, but it didn't change the fact that I still missed Ayushi, the actual daughter of Naresh uncle and Deepika aunty. She died in a road accident," Kajal said.

I saw her taking a deep breath.

"It's not easy, it wouldn't have been, even for me if I went away with strangers, but maybe it's the parental vibe Chahat got from Naresh uncle and Deepika aunty, that she agreed to come to America. Chahat was always sweet and adjusting towards whatever life threw at her. She took it all with a smile. She's a fighter and also a survivor," Kajal said.

I nodded. She really was. Chahat was a very strong girl.

"But one day, I went to their home and I was about to knock on her door when I heard her saying 'I loved you and I'll always love you.' That's the time I got to know that she was lying when she had said she's single and she was lying every time she said she never loved anyone," Kajal said.

I closed my eyes, taking it all in.

"I tried to find who it was, but I failed, until you came into our lives. Isn't it weird that now when I know who the guy is, I realise it's the same guy who I love?" Kajal said.

I opened my eyes and looked at Kajal.

She loves me?!

"But it doesn't matter. What actually matters is the one you love, and you know, the girl you love is a fighter and a survivor, but she also is stubborn. She is in a habit of putting others' happiness before her, and that's why she is keeping my happiness first. She doesn't know it is okay to let yourself be happy," Kajal said.

"Kajal—" I started, but she cut me off.

"Aryan, I know she's the one you have loved and still love, and I know you're the one she still loves with everything in her. Don't let anyone come in between. Don't let any circumstance take your love away from you, again. Go and make her yours," Kajal said, tears dropping from her eyes.

"But what about you?" I asked.

"Me? Aryan, I love you and I love your smile. As much as I want to be yours, I know I am not the one who could keep that smile on your face. It's Chahat and only Chahat," Kajal said, smiling despite the falling tears.

I hugged Kajal tightly.

"Thank you so much, Kajal. Thanks a lot. If it weren't for you, maybe I would have let Chahat go yet again," I said.

I pulled back and smiled at her.

"Go. I'll handle everything here," Kajal whispered.

I nodded and almost ran to the door of the balcony.

"Aryan?" Kajal called after me.

"Yes?" I asked.

"All the best," Kajal shouted.

"Thank you, and Kajal, what's her room number?" I asked, feeling silly.

"That's 5006," Kajal replied, smiling amidst her tears.

"Thank you," I said smiling and ran towards Chahat's room.

I looked for her room and knocked hard.

Deepika aunty opened the door.

"Hey, is Ayushi in here?" I asked.

"No, Ayushi told me she had to attend some important meeting in America so she left," Deepika Aunty said.

"She left?" I asked, shocked.

"Yes," she said, shrugging.

I closed my eyes, nodding and when I opened my eyes again, something caught my attention. I looked past her and saw Chahat's chain that still had my ring in it. I took that chain with the ring in my hand.

"When did she leave?" I asked.

"Probably about twenty minutes back," she replied.

'I won't let you go away again, Chahat,' I thought as I kept the chain with that ring in my pocket and ran downstairs, calling my driver to get the car in front.

I sat in the car and immediately told the driver to drive towards the airport.

'I am leaving tomorrow. I can't take it. I'll die like this!'

I should have known! How could I forget this?

I really wish she hasn't checked in or it would be really difficult for me to find her.

I reached the airport in no time. I looked around and didn't see her. She had entered, probably.

"Sir, if you want to go beyond here, you have to show us your ticket," the guard said when I tried to enter.

"I don't have the ticket, but please let me enter," I said.

"No, we can't," he said.

"I'm Aryan Kapoor, from Kapoor group of industries. I'll cause no harm. I have to find someone. It's important. Just let me go in for a bit until I find the person," I said.

"Sir, I recognise you from all the media coverage over the years, but I am sorry, rules are the same for everyone. We are sorry," the guard said.

"You can't do this! She'll go away yet again!" I said.

"Sir, please step aside. We aren't stopping you. Get a ticket and we will let you in," he said.

"Why can't you understand? I just need that person and I don't want to go anywhere. Please, let me find that person and I'll come out. You can come with me too, but please let me enter," I said.

"No, sir. It's not really under my control. I can't do anything here," he said.

I sighed. He won't let me go inside and find her until I have a ticket. Just then, an idea struck me.

"Can you at least tell me whether you remember anyone checking in with the name Ayushi Chawla or Chahat Aggarwal or anyone who was going to leave for the US?" I asked.

He looked at me weirdly.

"Sir, I hope you know that I check many tickets and IDs and it's not possible for me to remember everyone's name and destination," he said.

"She must have been here like twenty minutes back. It's not a long time. Please try to remember," I said.

"Twenty minutes?" he asked.

"Yes, twenty minutes only," I said, feeling a hope.

"I don't think so," he said.

"Are you sure?" I asked.

"Pretty much, but not fully," he said.

Maybe a picture could help.

"This is what she looks like," I said, taking out my phone and showing him a picture of Chahat.

He looked at it for a minute.

"No, I don't think I saw her today," he said.

I nodded.

"Okay, thank you so much," I said, to which he nodded.

If she isn't here, then, where is she?

"Sir, if you want, I could inform you if she comes here?" the guard said.

"That would be amazing! Here, this is my number. You can give me a call on this number if you find her here," I said, giving him my card.

"Okay," he said, taking it.

"Thank you so much. You don't know how much you are helping me," I said, extremely grateful to him.

I heard someone calling my name. I turned around and saw Siddhant and Abhi coming towards me.

"You could have told us, asshole! Kajal told us what happened," Siddhant said.

"Guys, I didn't have the time," I said.

"It's not the time for this, guys. When did Chahat reach here, Aryan?" Abhi asked.

"Deepika aunty said she left twenty minutes back when I went to her room. But she is not here," I replied.

"Then where is she?" Abhi asked.

"She left the hotel saying she has a flight to catch, but she isn't at the airport. Then where has she gone?" Siddhant wondered out loud.

"There's only one place left where she could go now," I said, hopeful.

"Where?" Abhi and Sid asked.

"You'll know," I said as we sat in my car and I told the driver where to go.

Chahat

"Mom, I have to leave," I said as she entered my hotel room.

"What? Why?" she asked.

"Actually, I got an e-mail saying there's an important meeting in office and since Kajal can't attend that, I have to go," I said as I zipped my last bag.

"That's another issue, but are you alright? You have eye bags," She said.

"Yes. It's just that I didn't sleep yesterday," I lied.

"Are you sure?" she asked, concerned.

"Yes, mom. I am sure. Don't worry," I said and she smiled at me.

"My dearest daughter, take care and we'll be there with you in a couple of days," she said.

"Already? You had to come a few days later," I said.

"We can't leave our daughter like that, can we?" she asked and I smiled at her.

She has always been like this – kind, loving and caring towards me.

I went to the washroom and freshened up. I was washing my hands, when I looked at myself in the mirror and my eyes fell on the chain around my neck that had the ring in it. Aryan's ring. Aryan is getting married to Kajal today. Now, Kajal was the only one who deserved to have Aryan's ring on her finger or around her neck. It wasn't me. I closed my eyes and slowly removed the chain from my neck. When Mom was tapping on her phone, I used the moment to keep the chain on the table.

"I'm all set to leave," I said as I took my handbag and my suitcase.

She stood up and hugged me tightly.

"Be safe, my dear," she said and kissed my forehead.

I nodded and smiled at her. I then left my room and went down to the lobby.

'I'm pretty sure I'll get a taxi outside,' I thought as I moved out.

I spotted a taxi nearby and told the address to the driver. I sat back and looked outside the window, reliving all the beautiful memories I had made in Mumbai. I remembered the time when we came to Aryan's house. I was on the verge of crying when Mary hugged me and I felt I was hugging someone from my past. I felt as if I could live the life I left behind five years back. It felt as if I wasn't Ayushi, but Chahat again.

"Ma'am, we are here," the driver said.

I looked at the sight in front of me. The same sight I had craved to see for the past five years. The sight I just saw in the pictures I had in my phone.

I got out of the car. The taxi left and I turned around to enter my home. The home where I had millions of memories with my mom, my brother and dad. The home where I grew up. The home which witnessed my family in its best and the worst phases. I was scared to come there earlier, because I knew I would cry and break down. But now that I was face to face with the bitter reality of my life, I knew that I had to move on and to move on, I had to face my fears.

I moved near the door and was shocked to see the door still so clean. That's not how I had expected to see it. I thought it would have been covered in dirt. The grass in the garden looked great, like it was watered from time to time. I felt someone was moving inside. I stood on the side and just then, two men came out and they looked like housekeepers by their uniforms.

"No one lives here and still he tells us to clean this place every week," one housekeeper said, sighing.

"Yes, but the one he loved used to live here," the other one reminded.

I immediately knew Aryan got this place cleaned every week.

I moved to the back of the house and found the spot near the flowers where our family hid one extra house key in case of emergency. I moved my hands there and got hold of the house key. I came to the front and opened the door and walked in.

I entered my home and everything was in its proper place, clean. There even were fresh flower garlands on the photos of my parents. Although it did not have its old homely vibe, but being back somehow felt like I was home. I was at the place where my heart and soul belonged.

I moved around, reliving the memories, crying a bit and laughing a bit, before I went to my room and opened my cupboard. I moved aside my clothes and found my diary lying there.

I went down to the living room and sat on the couch. I took out a pen and started writing.

Dear diary,

Destiny knows how to surprise one. Each surprise opens doors. One door which leads to new opportunities and the other one which leads to a new misery. It's all on us which door we choose to walk into.

As I remember now, we never had the most romantic first talk, but still this moron named Aryan managed to make my heart skip a beat. How his smile managed to make me blush was beyond my comprehension. Stupid moments had meaning when those were spent with him. Lame jokes turned funny when they came from him. Wasting time turned into memories when it was with him. How he did that is still beyond my understanding.

It was somewhere between crying just at the thought of losing him, getting sad when I saw he was low or taking care of him when he was sick, and telling him every detail of my day, that I realised I fell in love with him.

Time passed so quickly with him that I didn't realise how things turned around, how destiny threw bad news at me and I found myself transformed into someone I hated the most.

Time after that went on so painfully slow that I could live every pain of my life. With new people, a new country and without the one I love, who had no clue of where I was – destiny surprised me.

I cursed myself, I hated myself for what I had done and I was remorseful. All I wanted then was to be with him and only him. I craved his warmth, his cologne, his smile, his presence. I prayed for him.

But not every prayer is answered. Indeed, god planned such a funny destiny for me that today, despite being a few minutes away from him, I can't be with him.

He was the smile I smiled. He was the breath I took in.

How do I live when my breath was going to belong to someone else? How?

Despite loving each other with all our hearts, despite promising to have a happily ever after, despite standing like a rock beside each other in every up and down of our life, our love still remains misty and out of our reach!

I wrote the last sentence and tears fell from my eyes. I closed my eyes with fresh tears still on my cheeks and the diary in my hands. I got so engrossed in my thoughts that I didn't hear the car pulling up or the door of the house opening. All I was focussed on was getting some peace and relishing the last moments I was spending in my home. These moments would never come back.

"Chahat," a voice said. Aryan!

I chuckled to myself.

"Wow. Now I'm hallucinating too," I muttered out loud.

"Chahat, you aren't hallucinating. I am here," Aryan said and I still couldn't believe my ears.

I opened my eyes and found Aryan kneeling in front of me while I sat on the couch. He was kneeling with teary eyes and untidy hair. I couldn't believe my eyes.

Aryan is here? How? He is supposed to be at his wedding.

I slowly moved my hand up and kept it softly on his cheek. His eyes closed at the touch and that's then we realised that I had touched him like that after five years.

"I missed this. I missed you," he said with his eyes closed. I nodded.

"What are you doing here?" I asked slowly after a few minutes and took my hand back.

He opened his eyes and looked at me. He kept his hands on mine and smiled at me, and for the first time after five years, I saw his smile reaching his eyes.

"I'm here to take you back and make you mine. Chahat, I am here and you're here and today the world is with us. Now, nothing can stop me from making you mine forever. I love you, Chahat. I love you the most. I lost my smile, my happiness, my reason to live. I lost myself when you left. You're my entire world, my entire universe," he said.

My heart swelled at his words.

"Still? After knowing about my past?" I asked.

"Chahat, I know your heart. I know what you did was not intentional. And why would I stop loving you after knowing this? This thing happened just to test my love and we both know that my love for you is too strong to be affected by this. Chahat, I mean it when I say I love you," he said.

"Aryan, it's not so easy. I stayed away from you because I was remorseful. We both know how much I love you, but it doesn't change the fact that I can't let go of my past. I can't. I hate myself," I said.

"Chahat—" he started but he was cut off.

"Chahat," a voice came from the door.

I looked up to see Kajal standing there with a smile on her face. She came and sat down beside me.

"Chahat, I guess you both are just the same. You both think too much. I feel I need to put some sense into your head just like I did to this man," Kajal said and chuckled.

"Chahat, as you know, I had never been in love before this man," she said with eyes on Aryan and my eyes widened a tad bit.

Kajal loves Aryan?

"Okay, don't kill me for that and let me continue. I thought I would keep him happy and that maybe he loved me back, but I was wrong. I was heartbroken after I overheard your conversation last night, but suddenly, all I wanted to do was give him his happiness. It didn't matter whether it was me or some other girl and breaking my own heart for his happiness was not a big deal. Instead, it gave me happiness. I don't know what kind of love this is but I wanted him to have you because you are his smile, you are his happiness," Kajal said.

"So, Miss Aggarwal, I am not here for you, but I am here for myself, because I want the two people I love, Aryan and you, to find their way back to each other. Chahat, you stubborn girl, I know how you put others' happiness before yours and you do it because you feel you don't deserve it, but let me tell you, you are a pure soul and you deserve to be happy. Just think how much you have sacrificed in the past five years! You aren't selfish! If you were, you would have gone back to Aryan and not stayed with those suffering parents. Not everyone has the ability to accept their mistakes and repent about them; only strong-willed and kind people have this ability and you're one of them," Kajal said.

"You know what, seeing you like this is breaking the heart of your parents and of Ayushi. You didn't know her, but I did. I knew her too well and I know making others unhappy to make herself happy was a no-no for her. She was just like you – selfless, kind and loving. For once, Chahat, for once, accept that you deserve happiness, you deserve love just like every human being.

You're a human who makes mistakes. All you need is a person who loves you despite all these mistakes and you have him. Look at him, he's ready to put the world at your feet. Please, forgive yourself and love yourself. Accept yourself, your flaws just like Aryan did. Please," Kajal said, again.

I looked at her and then at Aryan.

"Please, Chahat. Give me my Chahat back. Don't make me suffer more. I don't know how I'll survive if you leave me again. Please Chahat," Aryan said.

My eyes became watery. I looked at my lap and saw Aryan's hands lying on top of mine.

Should I give myself a chance to be happy? Should I accept the fact that I have suffered too much and I deserve to be loved and I deserve to love? Is it true that by being sad, I am breaking my parents' and Ayushi's hearts?

I looked up and saw Aryan's red eyes. I knew I promised myself to give him someone pure but also someone who would give him all the happiness of the world and maybe it's only me who could give it to him.

I smiled at Aryan and it was evident how his eyes were surprised at first, but then shone with happiness.

He raised his eyebrows as if asking if it was a 'yes' to which I nodded with a smile on my face. He smiled the biggest smile he could possibly muster and hugged me tightly. I hugged him back and couldn't help but cry.

"I love you, Chahat. I am so happy to finally have you back in my arms. I can't believe this is happening," he said and I knew he was crying more than I was.

"I love you too much, Aryan. I... I thought I lost you forever. I thought we won't ever be able to be like this again," I said and hugged him tightly for what felt like forever.

We pulled apart and suddenly, Aryan stood up and held out his hand for me to take. I looked at him confused but stood up after placing my diary aside. He held my hand tightly and took me in front of my parents' photo. He made me face him and got down on one knee.

He took out my ring from his pocket again and my hand went to my mouth.

"Chahat Agarwal, after five years, we are back here, in front of your parents. Maybe destiny isn't as cruel as we imagined it to be. All these years have tested our love for each other and these years are proof that two people who are meant to be, will always find their way back to each other, no matter how much time passes, no matter how much distance they have and no matter what circumstances they are in. So, Chahat Aggarwal, after five years, once again, will you please be mine forever? Will you marry me?" Aryan said, making me cry, but after many years, I was crying out of sheer happiness and not of misery, heartache and guilt.

"I will. Oh my god, I love you! I will marry you," I said and put my hand forward and he slid the ring on my finger again and got up.

We hugged each other tightly and kissed each other. It was full of the love we had for each other. It was as if we had found our oxygen back, our home back, our happiness, our life, our love back.

How much I love this man!

"Guys, I am still here," Kajal's voice came and we pulled apart and looked at her. She was covering her eyes and we laughed.

"Thank you so much, Kajal, for everything you did for us," I said.

"Ugh! You both are forgetting your lines. I was only a medium, but now I truly believe that when two people love each other honestly, they will, no matter what happens, always find a bright future," she said.

I nodded and looked at Aryan who was already looking at me.

"I love you, Mrs Kapoor," he said.

"I love you so much more. We both are lucky because we, somehow, managed to finish our chase, to be with each other forever," I said, smiling and with this he sealed my lips with his once again.